# Dutch Color

# Dutch Color

Douglas M. Jones III

MOSCOW, IDAHO

*Canon Press*

Douglas M. Jones III, *Dutch Color*

Published by Canon Press, P.O. Box 8729, Moscow, ID 83843
800-488-2034 / www.canonpress.org

© 2000 by Douglas M. Jones III

04 03 02 01 00  /  9 8 7 6 5 4 3 2 1

Cover design by Paige Atwood Design, Moscow, ID

Printed in the United States of America.

*Library of Congress Cataloging-in-Publication Data*

Jones, Douglas, 1963–
      Dutch color / Douglas Jones.
      p.   cm.
Summary: In seventeenth-century Holland, a young woman vows to solve the mystery of her father's disappearance following a voyage to Venice to obtain paint color recipes for the painters of Utrecht.
      ISBN 1-885767-65-X (pbk.)
      [1. Fathers—Fiction. 2. Missing persons—Fiction. 3. Artists—Fiction.
      4. Painting, Dutch—Fiction. 5. Netherlands—Fiction.] I. Title.
      PZ7.J6853 Du 2000
      [Fic]—dc21                                                    00-009414

For my sisters,
Berta and Lucy.

Thanks for all the childhood
torture and laughter,
especially the laughter.

# Table of Contents

TRAIECTUM

*The city of Utrecht around the time of this story*

# CHAPTER ONE

# Beach Flop

"It's not this one. No. It smells too much like fish," Clara said. Her fingers thoughtlessly toyed with the fabric of her brother's sleeve.

Their Uncle Caspar stared out over the harbor from under the broad brim of his dark hat, but Uncle Hendrick tilted his head and looked over his spectacles at the wooden bulk sitting in front of the four of them; it was a common Dutch *fluit* ship, newly built that year, 1629.

"Well, it is a *fishing* boat," Uncle Hendrick said. He stared at the back of Clara's head, speaking as if to a slightly mad dog. "And this *is* a harbor. Everything here is required to smell like fish. Even my new jacket *now*, thanks to you." His words poked holes through the lingering smoke of his pipe.

"Please, *please,* Uncle, don't say that word," Clara said, not taking her eyes off the boat.

"Which word?"

No answer.

He exaggerated his lips, guessing. "Fishing?" He spoke it crookedly.

"Stop it. Please stop." Clara wiggled her skinny arms and kept her attention on the sailors walking down the boat ramp onto the dock.

Uncle Hendrick raised his eyebrows to his brother Caspar. Uncle Caspar reached into his coat and pulled out an imaginary notebook. He opened it and pretended to write. His broad white collar stood stiff as he moved.

"I'm afraid, Hendrick, we have to slay yet another word. Let's see what other banned words are on the list in front of it. There's *bugle* and *moist* and *Amsterdam* and *lips* and . . ."

Clara covered her ears and tilted her head straight back in order to see him. She mouthed the words "You are cruel" and turned back to the boat.

"I want to go ask them," Clara said and grabbed her brother's hand as she started down the dock. At eight, Ernst was almost as tall as Clara was at thirteen. But Ernst wanted nothing to do with these sailors.

"No, Clara, I want to go see that whale." He peeled her grip from his hand and ran back to their two uncles. She didn't pause but kept walking right up the gangplank, her deep blue skirt swishing against the men. On the back of her head she wore a colorfully embroidered cap that fit closely to her pinned hair. Her head barely reached the sailors' barreled chests. One sailor teased at her cap with his heavy fingers. Her blond arm snapped out and slapped at his hand.

When she reached the top, Clara cupped her hands around her mouth. "I'm looking for my father!"

"I'm looking for mine!" shouted back one sailor.

"I'm your father!" said another. Others laughed.

"We fed him to the fish," said one.

"We ate him," said another. They laughed again.

Clara put her hands on her hips. "I'm not laughing," she said.

"We are," the last sailor said.

"I'm surprised you know how to talk!" She shot off the words into the air after them.

From behind her came a slow, deep voice. "Watch

your mouth, missy." The captain had just walked up. Turning, she collided with him and flinched at his bulk.

"Sorry, Captain," Clara said. Her uncles were already running up the gangplank to her, their hats removed from their heads.

"Please, excuse her, captain," said Uncle Hendrick, sort of bowing. "She's really not well. Too many strawberries, I'm afraid."

Uncle Caspar stepped in too. "She's from Utrecht. Everyone there is a little . . . you know . . ." He pulled his ear and opened his mouth wide.

They hustled her down the plank, half carrying her, half pushing; her shoes thudded on the dock a few times. Uncle Caspar whispered, "It's not good to pick fights with water gorillas."

Uncle Hendrick nodded. "Especially if you're just a ribbon of a girl." They reached the bottom. "Now, Caspar and I could flatten them all."

Caspar nodded to Hendrick. "Yes, we could indeed if we were entirely different men."

"Yes, of course, entirely different," said Hendrick.

"Wait!" she said, and she stiffened her body more. "I want to speak to the captain." She wriggled free and turned. "Captain! My father left this city . . . Amsterdam"—she cringed to say that word—"eight months ago for Venice, Italy. He's five months late. He would have been carrying color mixes as cargo. Have you seen him?"

The captain didn't look at her. "I've seen too many Dutchmen going to Italy. Every painter goes. They are a blur."

She shrugged her shoulders twice and pushed a loose strand of her hair back over her ear. She breathed heavily through her nose.

"Maybe Father is looking at that whale," said Ernst, trying to sneak that topic back to her attention. He made a weird face to make her laugh.

"Come on," he said, "we'll miss it." Clara ruffled his hair and sighed in resignation.

Far down from the dock, a crowd shouted and hooted. Some were laughing, others were making warning sounds. Ernst pulled his sister's arm. "It's the whale, I tell you. They will chop it up, and we won't have seen it."

With that thought, Ernst broke into a gallop, and Clara followed close behind, not wanting to miss any excitement. Away they went, down the dock, along the beach road. Amsterdam was made up of intricate paths of canals, strips of land, and quay walls where ships were moored. A small tip of sandy beach jutted out from one side of the harbor.

Even though the uncles kept saying a beached whale was a bad omen, the two men slowly followed the children. As they all moved farther away from the dock, the smell of fish began to mingle more with that of fresh bread. In the distance they could see the giant crowd standing in a half-circle on the small beach. Ernst ran on ahead of his sister and uncles. He could smell the dead whale before he saw it—the smell of boiling cabbage mixed with eggs drying in sunshine. The whale had beached itself two days before, and it had long since died. Ernst had hoped to see it breathe.

When he reached the inner crowd he noticed that people kept well away from the grand pile of whale laying on its side. He pushed and squeezed between big legs to fill his eyes with whale. Ernst looked up and couldn't see over the top of the whale to the crowd on the other side. Before him was a mountain of dry gray, dotted with barnacles. Some men had tightened ropes across the whale, making it look striped. Its skinny jaw sat open at an odd angle. Several long triangles came out of its sides. Ernst didn't know what those were; maybe they were sails. The people on the outer edge spoke loudly. The people along the inner edge, closest to the whale, stood in complete silence, as if at a king's funeral. When clusters of people could no longer stand the rotting smell, they would leave the front row and move away silently through the crowd, shaking their heads and muttering about divine curses.

Ernst finally closed his mouth when his sister came up behind him. She put her hands on his head like a little cap. Clara's eyes followed the men inserting hooks into the whale and wrapping ropes around it. They were either going to turn it over or try to drag it out to sea. Several boys had also been climbing up the ropes, getting in the way. The sailors kept swishing them away, but like gnats, the boys would scatter for a moment and then return. Clara pushed Ernst's head forward.

"Why don't you go climb it?" she said.

Ernst pretended for a moment not to hear her. Then he answered, "One of the boys got stuck. His leg popped through the dry whale skin."

"I think," Clara said, "you should go to the top and give a speech."

Ernst paused. "I would, but I can't remember anything right now."

"Do your catechism," she said. He clicked his tongue.

"I was too little the last time a whale beached here," she said. "I'm not going to miss my ride this time." She vanished. A few moments later, Ernst heard shouting on the other side of the whale. He could see that someone was pulling on the ropes from the other side, and he just knew it would be his sister. He stood grinning, waiting for Clara's head to appear over the top of the whale.

Finally, there she was. Her cap had come off. She steadied herself and stood tall. The sunshine danced within the gold tangles of her hair, loosened in places.

"That's my sister," Ernst said to those around him. He waved both hands at her. She waved back and made a big "O" with her mouth. Several boys followed her up and sat around her feet.

She took a deep breath; her balance slipped a bit. She took another big breath and shouted, "Quiet, please! Quiet! I have a famous poem for this occasion:

> My brush is my sword; my broom my weapon!
> Sleep I know not, nor any repose!
> No labor is too heavy; no care too great!
> To make everything shine and spotlessly neat!
> I scrape and scour; I polish and scrub!
> And suffer no one to take my tub!"

A few people clapped. Most were watching the sailor crawling up behind her. The boys saw him and scattered, sliding down. She curtseyed to the crowd and then shouted, "I am the whale queen! Please clap your hands above your head for me, Clara Zoelen!"

A few started clapping and laughing, then more. Soon all the people in the crowd were clapping their hands above their heads. Clara smiled. "Thank you. *I am* the whale queen!"

The sailor finally reached her. He wasn't smiling. He grabbed her by the waist and flopped her over his shoulder. She didn't object. She stretched out her hands to the crowd once more and started singing "I am the whale queen!" over and over. Once the sailor and Clara reached the sand, she curtseyed to him and raced off into the crowd, sand flying behind her.

Down on the other side of the whale, Ernst looked at the people staring at him. "My sister is the whale queen," he said and went off to find her.

Clara and Ernst met at the uncles, who had waited alongside the beach road. Their backs were to the whale, just so they could be contrary. Ernst hugged his sister.

"You missed it," said Ernst. He was out of breath. "Clara climbed the whale!"

Uncle Hendrick frowned and rolled his eyes. "Yes, and tulips give milk, I suppose."

Uncle Caspar shook his head. "No one can climb a whale. It's too slippery."

"*She* did!" said Ernst. "And look. Sailors are on it." The uncles and the children turned and peered over the crowd. No one was on the whale.

"Well, they *were* on it, and so was Clara!"

The uncles turned away from the whale. "Laughter and jokes," said Uncle Caspar. "Just forget it. We just won't fall for this one. Next you'll tell us the English can cook."

Uncle Hendrick chimed in, "Or that they can paint."

"Absurd," said Uncle Caspar. Ernst started to protest again, but Clara called him off with a shrug. She knew she had been on the whale.

The uncles started walking away. "Nevertheless," said Uncle Hendrick, "now that you're both finished staring at that dead-omen thing, let's make our way back through town, shall we?"

Crossing several canals, they made their way back to the main part of Amsterdam. On either side, houses and shops towered above them, until they came into the open area in the cathedral square. Merchants and shoppers spread out from there in all directions.

Uncle Caspar pulled out his coin purse. He put six guilders in Clara's hands. This was quite a lot of money for normal things, but not much for tulip bulbs. He nudged Uncle Hendrick in the side, encouraging him to contribute to the gift.

Uncle Hendrick shook his head. "No thank you, Caspar, I don't need any money."

Uncle Caspar nudged his arm. "I was suggesting that you chip in a coin or two. It wouldn't hurt."

"It might hurt *me*," said Uncle Hendrick. "This girl here would probably waste it on something wonderful and exquisite, like tulips." He shook his head. "I will contribute only if she agrees to buy something sense-less, like a pretzel. Moderation in all things, I say—only don't be extreme in your moderation."

Clara rubbed her head on Uncle Hendrick's sleeve like a cat. "Oh, Uncle, but pretzels don't call my name when I walk by. Tulips sing for attention. When they don't get that attention they turn nasty."

"They're choir beggars; don't trust them," said Uncle Hendrick. "That's all we need back home, more lazy flowers soaking up all the attention . . . Here." He put more coins in her hand. "Just be sure to get me two yellow-lion bulbs." Clara thanked him profusely and kissed his hand. Then he added, "And do save some of that money for the canal ride back to Utrecht."

He straightened his coat. "Now which flower mer-chant shall we visit first?" Clara leaned over to her brother and whispered in his ear.

"Come now," Uncle Hendrick repeated, "where shall we go?"

"*We?*" Clara echoed. She and Ernst looked at each other, turned, and ran off down the street, leaving the uncles behind. Within moments, the children were out of sight, lost amid the buyers and sellers. The uncles stood there, staring down the road, then at each other.

"Hmmm. I do believe they've abandoned us all alone here in Amsterdam," said Uncle Hendrick.

Uncle Caspar puffed out his lips in thought and shook his head. "But I'm not afraid," he said quickly.

"No, no, neither am I," said Uncle Hendrick. "But shouldn't we do something parental like find them or worry a bit?"

"I suppose so, but I'm too tired to worry."

"Perhaps we should call in some mercenary soldier-types with large weapons to hunt them down and blip them on their heads," said Hendrick.

"No, the soldiers might decide to hurt us instead," said Caspar.

"Yes, indeed; we can't trust mercenaries," said Hendrick. After a moment, he said, "I have just the idea."

Clara and Ernst ran around a corner and leaned against a stone wall. Their chests heaved up and down in quick breaths and laughter. After a moment Ernst said they should go back, or they'd never find the uncles; Clara said they shouldn't.

"We'll find them waiting for us at the canal boats. Come, let's go exploring," said Clara.

Ernst started walking back. "I thought we were just going to run away and then go back to them. Gypsies might snatch us," he said.

"Don't be silly," said Clara. "We know our way around this city just fine. We've been here at least sixty times. And there aren't any gypsies here." She rolled her eyes.

"Then sailors might steal us off to India," Ernst said, and he stepped back, turned, and ran off the way they had come, pushed by his fear. Clara waited right there. She knew. Within moments, Ernst came running back to her. "The uncles are gone!" he called, waving his arms high; his eyes glistened a bit.

"Good," said Clara. "Now we can get some proper tulips. Hurry along. You can pretend to be my French slave. I might even buy you a pretzel."

The two of them wandered in and around the market stalls. Ernst was sure he saw gypsies. Clara quickly bought him a large pretzel. It calmed him while she talked to the tulip sellers. She was searching for some special tulip colors. And she wanted the kind that she could plant now, just before the beginning of spring, the sort that would blossom in summer. She couldn't stand waiting for them through winter. Ernst was starting to lag. Clara kept promising that she was almost finished, though she hadn't yet purchased any bulbs.

Just when she herself was starting to lag, she stumbled upon a tulip seller offering a "mystery pick" of tulip bulbs. He had filled a halved wine cask with common, unexciting bulbs, but then with much fanfare in front of the crowd he took a rare Soomerschoon (SOE-mer-skone) tulip bulb from his top shelf and mixed it in with the common bulbs. Even common bulbs were expensive— about one guilder—which was about the price of five loaves of rye bread or ten pounds of cheese. A single Soomerschoon bulb cost about seventy guilders, or about three-hundred-and-fifty loaves of bread or seven-hundred pounds of cheese or three months wages for a bricklayer.

And yet, these weren't the most expensive bulbs. The most expensive bulbs, like the most famous of them all—the Semper Augustus—cost thousands of guilders. Every year the cost of tulip bulbs increased. Her uncles had told her that if this continued, someday a Semper Augustus would be more valuable than a house. They would be right.

To take a chance on the barrel, a chance on winning a seventy-guilder Soomerschoon, one had to pay the price of five common bulbs in order to select any three, and one might be the rare Soomerschoon bulb. In this way, the vendor could quickly get rid of his aging common bulbs.

Clara bit her lip. Even after buying the pretzel she had just enough to pay the mystery barrel price. When it came her turn, she handed over her money. The tulip seller made her turn her head away when she reached inside the barrel. She was sure she could "see" the Soomerschoon with the tips of her fingers. One. Two. Three. She pulled out her three bulbs, but they all looked the same. It was hard to tell if one was special. She plopped them into her skirt pockets and gave Ernst an evil grin. She patted her treasure, then they ran off toward the canal boats heading back to Utrecht.

The sun had hidden part of itself behind the buildings of Amsterdam, and thick cold clouds were moving overhead. The Zoelen children ran over a low, broad-arched bridge, and Clara cupped her hand over the pocket in her skirt. The canal boats left just three times a day for the seven-hour ride back to Utrecht. But other canal boats left more often. They could even ride the smaller boats to go part of the way and catch up with the larger boats if they had to. One boat was just leaving as the children ran up to the landing, but another would be boarding soon.

They waited for the uncles, but no uncles were

around to be seen. They walked along the dock for a moment, when they heard their uncles' shouts. They turned and looked up the dock, the street, the canal bank but couldn't see them. The calls continued.

Ernst turned and looked at the boat which had left as they were arriving. He saw the uncles. He pulled Clara's arm and pointed. All life had left his face. The uncles were leaning on the back of the boat waving their pipes toward the children, wishing them a good trip. Eye for eye; abandonment for abandonment.

Clara yelled out, "You can't leave us. We spent all the money!"

The uncles were too far away to hear her. The children could only make out a few words through the uncle's laughter, like "you a lesson" and "use the money we gave you." The uncles were quite proud of themselves.

Ernst slumped against the railing, slowly sliding down to the wooden dock. Clara's mind was clicking. "Come on," she said. "Let's go sell these bulbs back to a tulip merchant." They ran back to the flower market, but no seller wanted to buy her bulbs. She went to stall after stall, even to the man from whom she had purchased them. He brushed away her pleas. They headed back to the canal dock. She decided to try to beg a ride back home, promising the boat driver more money when they arrived in Utrecht.

But when they crossed the final bridge and started down the steps, Clara's throat grew dry. She could feel the beat of blood in her fingers. The cold air sneaked in next to her skin. Money would now be useless. They had been gone for over an hour, and they had missed the final boat out of Amsterdam. All the canal boats were gone, and the dock was closed. Ernst wanted to yell, but he couldn't even speak.

"You did this," he whispered and slid down again to the dock. The tears started rolling down his cheeks.

"Don't you go soft on me now," Clara said, and she tried to pull him up by his jacket. She couldn't do it. She crouched down and got in close to his face. "You stop that crying. They'll think I'm caring for a little girl." Her face was pulled tight, but she couldn't stop her silent tears. They spilled out over her anger. She stood up; Ernst kept crying aloud. She crouched down with new energy and pulled up on his collar again. She had another idea. "Say the first catechism!" she told him, close to his eyes. She shook him. He couldn't. She banged him against the railing a bit. "Say the first catechism!" She was hissing now. "Say it! 'What is your only comfort in life and death?'" He grew quiet. She pushed him back again and lifted up his chin. "Answer me. 'What is your only comfort?'"

He spoke through his weeping. "That I with body and soul, both in life and death, am not my own, but belong unto my faithful Savior Jesus Christ; who with his precious blood—"

"That's enough. Say that part again," Clara said and pushed him back. He said it again, and she made him say it a third and fourth time. He had stopped crying by then. She stood and helped him up.

Ernst looked her in the eyes. "It's a catechism, not a magic potion," he said. "Don't make me say things you won't." She brushed dirt off of him but didn't answer.

She sighed for her father. Her brother made a loop with his arm, and she slid her arm through. As they slowly walked up the steps arm in arm, they realized that the sun had left them. A dark Amsterdam awaited.

# CHAPTER TWO

# Secret Election

As Clara and Ernst walked through the dark streets of Amsterdam, the flaming street torches twisted the children's shadows into monstrous shapes in front of them. Ernst kept spinning around, looking and waiting for the echo of his feet to die down. They turned to a faster pace and then ran.

"Where are we going?" asked Ernst.

"Don't talk, just run," said Clara. She looked back and saw some odd shadows down the street. She ran faster, listening for other footsteps. Ernst asked to stop. She made him keep running. She made her feet keep rhythm with her brother's steps and listened for off-beat steps. She was now sure there was something, other footsteps. They were getting louder. Maybe it was the uncles.

She looked over her shoulder, but it was too dark to see, and the uncles would have called out and couldn't have run for so long. The children turned a corner, and Clara pulled Ernst down under a wagon and put her hand over his mouth. Neither moved. They tried to slow their breathing. The footsteps came closer. It sounded like several men. The steps came to the corner and stopped.

From under the wagon Clara could see four dark shapes looking up and down the street. None of them were the uncles. The group of men split into two pairs and ran in different directions. Two men ran right by the wagon but seemed to stop after a few steps. Ernst started to turn his head to look, but Clara pulled him to her chest. They crouched in the darkness, but as their eyes got used to the pool of darkness it seemed to get lighter. Perhaps things were getting lighter for the two men as well.

The darkness that had at first been the children's protector was turning into a traitor. Clara had stopped breathing completely; the blood beat in her ears, her lungs burned. *Mother will kill us,* she thought. Clara covered her ears with her hands, not knowing what else to do.

The footsteps started again, but in which direction? The two men murmured to each other for a moment, then their walking turned into running, running away, down the street and around the corner. The children breathed out and glanced up and down the street. But the sound of running seemed to fade when the men passed the corner. Had they stopped? Were they waiting?

Clara pointed in the other direction, across the street toward a small park and whispered, "We have to get through there." Ernst nodded.

They looked up and down the street again and readied their legs for sprinting. Clara grabbed Ernst's hand and nodded. They crawled out from under the wagon and ran, but their steps were too loud. They instantly made their legs take long, quiet steps on tiptoe.

When they reached the park grass, they started running again. Some bushes got in their way, and Ernst ran headlong into them, tripping. Clara got him up and pointed to a building across the street. It was a church; its entry glowed with torchlight. They ran out onto the street, not trying to quiet their steps any longer, then up the church steps and pulled on the locked door; they pounded on its thickness. Roman Catholic doors would have been unlocked, but these were Protestant doors, locked during the week.

No one answered their pounding, and the doorway light revealed them to anyone who might be watching. They pounded more and looked back over their shoulders. Clara heard a voice from around the side of the doorway. She darted out and saw the pastor's wife at the door of the house next door. Clara grabbed her brother's arms which were still beating on the door and ran him to the squinting woman. When she saw that they were children, the woman didn't ask them any questions; she ushered them into her house and closed the door. The children whispered their story in torrents as the silver-haired wife seated them at her table. The tall pastor moved through the room without a word, but holding a dark club the length of his arm. He passed through the door, out into the street.

The uncles had waited for Clara and Ernst at the next canal-boat stop which was only twenty minutes up the canal. Plenty of boats zipped up and down the waterway, each easily catching up with the bigger boat that made the longer trek to Utrecht. But the children hadn't shown up on any of those boats. The uncles finally abandoned their big boat and took a smaller one back to Amsterdam. All along the way, they scanned the scene for the children.

"Why is it that your stupid jokes never work out?" Caspar asked without looking at Hendrick.

Hendrick kept leaning on the boat rail, staring at the dark water. Then he said, "You know, I don't seem to recall any objection back when I suggested it."

Caspar frowned and said, "Ahhh, but I have grown up some since then." A long silence settled between them.

Finally Uncle Hendrick said, "Don't worry. We'll find them."

But when they had reached Amsterdam, the children were nowhere to be found.

In the morning, ivory sunlight warmed the room where the children slept. Clara awakened to the smell of pastries. It pulled her up on her elbows, then to her extended arms, and then she sat upright. She ran her hand over the mountains of softness that was the guest bed. It reminded her of home. She got out and straightened the bed, smoothing the thick covers. Ernst was still asleep on the floor; she stepped over him and walked toward the kitchen area. She studied the high walls lined with paintings.

After the pastor's wife stuffed the children with pastries, Clara and Ernst thanked the couple again and again and said they had to start for home. The pastor refused to let them walk and insisted on taking them home to Utrecht on horseback, a very long trip. Ernst was glad he didn't have to walk. The three of them rode on one horse—the pastor, Clara, and Ernst, in order.

The road linking Amsterdam and Utrecht ran alongside a wide canal. On either side, nobles and wealthy merchants had built some of the most beautiful mansions in Holland. The mansions crouched like small castles, wrapped in gardens and windows and stone; all along the canal, elegant stone arches guarded their garden entrances.

Clara dreamed of someday living in one of them. She would paint away the days while her dark-haired husband tended horses, and their children ran around her garden and sometimes broke things.

After riding along the road to Utrecht for about an hour, they could see another horseman coming toward them. It was one man with two horses. The rider was very round, unlike their father. As the man approached, he waved his open hand in the air, and the Zoelen children recognized him by his bushy gray eyebrows as Romeyn Liebens, an acquaintance of their father's.

"I can't believe I have found you!" Mr. Liebens said, his giant smile was made bigger by sausage lips. He tried to get off his horse to greet them but realized it would take too much effort for him to climb up again.

The pastor pulled alongside him, and Mr. Liebens explained that the children's mother was terrified and had sent him out first thing that morning to find them. He said their mother was sure they were lying dead in some street in Amsterdam. The pastor explained what had happened. During all the talking, all Clara could think about was riding that second horse. It looked like chocolate.

"Why didn't the uncles come for us?" asked Ernst.

"We thought they were still with you." Mr. Liebens giggled and rubbed his fingers over his lips. "She asked that I come," he said and giggled again. "So come along. I've brought an extra horse for you two. Your uncles will have to find their own way."

Sister and brother both scrambled to get off the pastor's horse, each trying to sit up front on the new ride. Clara won. Nothing could have stood in her way. As they sat high upon that horse, the rest of the world blurred as if they were on a mountain. They almost forgot to thank the pastor, but Mr. Liebens signaled them with his eyes. After all the words had been spoken, Clara turned "her" horse around and galloped off. Mr. Liebens yelled at her to stop; she did. Since Liebens couldn't keep up, he allowed them to ride ahead for a short distance, then turn and ride back. They did this all the way to Utrecht.

They arrived at midafternoon and rode through the intricate streets of Utrecht, over the canals, to Steenweg, the street where they lived. They saw Mother standing in front of their townhouse, her arms folded. She was simply an older version of Clara—blond, slight, and sharp-edged. Mother always stood as if she were apologizing for being wherever she was, always a little jittery. Their tall house sat neatly side-by-side with others, and like those around it, its front rose high into a mustache curl of white wood and stone.

Clara laughed as she rode up to Mother. "You thought we were dead!"

Mother didn't speak. She stamped her foot and walked inside. Clara and Ernst dismounted and thanked Mr. Liebens, but as they headed in, Mr. Liebens signaled Clara to come back to his horse.

He leaned over. "I had hoped we could speak while we rode, but you insisted on flying that horse." Clara just smiled. He added, "I really must speak to you privately and soon."

Clara's head tilted. "Why not now?"

"Privately," he said slowly. "Why don't you meet me in your father's shop just before dark?" Clara shrugged and agreed. "But don't tell your mother or uncles or anyone. It must be our secret." He said "secret" with an exaggerated "s." Clara rubbed her arm, but she didn't let her face show her discomfort.

Mr. Liebens leaned down closer from the horse and whispered, "*I know where your father is.*" He giggled. Her eyes grew larger. Mr. Liebens tipped his hat and rode off quickly. She started to run after him, but he was gone. She stood alone in the street for a long while and then stamped her foot on the cobblestone.

Back in Amsterdam, the uncles had searched for Clara and Ernst most of the night. In the morning, they had checked with several pastors, asking if any of them had seen the children. At last the pastor who had helped the children explained that they had already returned to Utrecht by horse. The uncles decided that the canal boat would take too long, so they hired a carriage back to Utrecht and arrived several hours after their painting students had shown up for class. They didn't dare go by the Zoelen house. They went straight to class, as if nothing had happened.

Several hours later, Ernst burst in the front door and told Clara that painting class had been going on for some time.

Clara stared at Mother. "I have to go to the uncles," she pleaded. "Today's class is almost over. I can't miss it." Mother lectured Clara about frightening her to death and then coming home just to leave again.

"Please, Momma. The competition. They are working on the painting competition." Mother looked up at the ceiling and stared.

"Go, go," she said finally. Clara grabbed Mother's arm and kissed her elbow. She was gone.

Ernst was in the same class as Clara, so he darted out of the house too. When he was outside, he saw Clara already seven houses down, slowing her run and straightening her dress before entering the uncles' paint-ing studio.

"Well, Miss Zoelen, you are *quite* late," said Uncle Hendrick in Latin. Eleven boys dressed in black turned their heads from their sketch easels to look at her. Ernst came in behind her.

She replied in Latin, "*Magister* painter, I do have a solid excuse for being late." The boys in the class started making clicking noises. Uncle Hendrick waited. "I was detained in Amsterdam on business." She took her place behind her easel and started sketching the big plaster statue of a hand displayed in the center of the room.

"What sort of business?" Uncle Hendrick asked.

"It seems that the magistrates of Amsterdam are seeking two brothers who abandon children to become gypsies." She let the phrase float there for a moment. "They are quite upset. Apparently, there is quite a stiff fine for such things, and they asked me whether I knew anything about these two scoundrels. I just had to help them out."

For just a moment, the blood left the faces of the uncles. Clara continued sketching without raising her eyes.

"Oh, is that all?" asked Uncle Hendrick. "I thought you were going to tell us some tale about being the 'Whale Queen' who had to return to her people."

Clara's head snapped up to meet his gaze. She shook her torso ever so slightly. *The uncles had heard me from the whale!* she realized. Just then the other boys started chanting something very quietly at first, under their breaths. The vague sounds took on edges, going from "eh ee" to "ell een" to "Whale Queen! Whale Queen! Whale Queen!"

The uncles stood in the background. The boys left

their easels and danced around Clara as she quietly sketched, behaving as if she were in a spring garden all by herself. Ernst just sat smiling behind his easel.

The students would have gone on chanting forever, but the uncles finally shouted them down. Clara kept sketching intently. All the boys were finally back at their easels, only slightly able to concentrate on the plaster hand model.

"Well, for those students who were so notoriously late," said Uncle Caspar, "we started the day grinding colors—blues and yellows—then we sketched a dog, a Caesar bust, a wheel, and now this Davidic hand. I think it looks something like mine, don't you? Anyway, the sketching and painting competition isn't far away, and we will select only five of you to compete. And only the best. It would be so wrong for you to embarrass us. As always, we want to see you think in terms of *houding* (HOW-ding). We know you're sniveling art rats and that most of you will never understand *houding*, but we have to start somewhere. Remember that *houding* is what?"

The students droned back, "the melody of painting." They had heard this speech a thousand times.

Uncle Caspar walked while he spoke. "*Houding* forces solids upon us with perfect shadowing. It harmonizes colors according to their powers. It perfects rounded space. Without *houding* your sketches and paintings will be what?"

"As dead as English cooking," they chanted.

Uncle Caspar walked behind the boys and examined their sketches as they worked with black chalk. "You remember that first prize is a Bartolomeo Manfredi painting, the disciple of Caravaggio. Quite a treasure, I must say. I would be willing to sell a small child for it myself, if I had one." He picked some debris off the plaster hand.

Clara had once seen three Manfredi paintings side by side and remembered feeling weak in front of them. She imagined her bedroom glowing like a furnace with a Manfredi on the wall. *No one will stop me,* she heard her herself say. She sketched steadily, then stared at her sketch and leaned forward. She licked a smudge across it with her tongue. That meant she hated it. She started over but ended up licking the next one, too. The third she liked better, and it survived unlicked.

After a time Uncle Hendrick observed, "We're starting to lose our sun. I think we should call it a day. Anyone finished with the hand?" No one spoke. Most of them had been working on their sketches for over an hour. "We must work much faster for the competition. This won't do."

Then someone said in a soft voice, "I'm done."

The uncles looked for the source of the remark.

"I'm done," said Clara more loudly. The other students groaned. She smiled wide and shrugged an apology.

"The Whale Queen claims to be finished," said Uncle Caspar. "You just got here a while ago. I'm sure it's rubbish," he said from across the room.

Uncle Hendrick walked over to examine Clara's work. He rolled his eyes. He knew what to expect. He had been here before. It was perfect. He beamed. "I knew it! What can I say boys? Sketching is in the family blood." He held it up and showed it off. Most of the boys didn't even look at it. They knew. Ernst squinted at it from across the room. Then he looked at his own sketch which resembled some sort of dried octopus. He mumbled something about blood.

The students started putting away their materials. Uncle Hendrick leaned over to Clara.

"You know, as punishment for being so late to class, I was hoping you might be willing to watch Roelof (REW-loff) for me tonight. Aunt Griet and I would like to go out visiting." Clara smiled as she packed her things.

"Is that all you have to say? Nothing about Amsterdam?" she asked.

"Oh, that . . . yes, yes, I forgive you," he said, nodding his head.

"You forgive me?" She laughed. "Momma's going to have both of your heads." But Clara didn't push the point too hard. She knew she was, after all, the one who had spent her canal boat money on tulips.

"Yes, well," Uncle Hendrick remarked, "humor demands risk and all that." Then he went on without a beat. "So will you watch Roelof for us tonight?"

Clara answered, "This week I call Roelof *Mr. Toopy*. And I will watch him if I can do it in Father's shop."

"That's fine. Just don't return him painted red this time."

Clara breathed a mock sigh. "He started off forest green and that was an accident," she said. "Then I decided he would make a delightful tulip, and I added the other colors to his head. But I assure you, I learned my lesson, and I won't be overcome again." She paused. "Though I do owe you for that abandonment thing," she said, twirling her fingers in the air.

"I'm sure you will repay. That's the only holy thing to do. Vengeance is yours, after all," said Uncle Hendrick. "But remember, moderation in all things."

She exaggerated a smile in reply. "But don't be extreme in your moderation," she added.

• • •

After dinner that night, Clara took the the hand of three-year-old Pudge or Mr. Toopy or Miguel or whatever she decided to call him other than his real name—Roelof. Uncle Hendrick's son walked slowly, dragging his feet.

"Will you please let me carry you?" she said.

"No," he said and made an 'x' in her face with his arms. "I'm hungry," he said.

"No, *what*, Mr. Toopy?" she asked. He pushed out his lips in silence.

Finally he said, "No, *Princess*."

"That's right," she said. "Don't forget it now."

Clara sat down at her father's main desk and ran her fingers over some of his tools, wondering where he could be at that very moment. The two of them had sat together in this shop for uncountable hours. He would always leave his work when she came in and turn his blue eyes to her. They had talked about painters, colors, history, and theology long into the night, their conversations always soaked in laughter. That's what she missed most—her father's laugh. It provided a place to stand boldly.

Above the desk, against the wall, sat piles of color recipe manuscripts—ice green, burgundy, mustard yellow. He had sailed to Venice, the color capital of the world, in search of new colors for Utrecht painters. He kept the most secret recipes hidden somewhere, perhaps with Mother, perhaps buried under floor stones, perhaps in plain sight to trick with the obvious. *Will he ever touch this desk again? He's probably lying cold off some Italian highway, beaten blue by robbers,* she thought.

"No," she said. "Mother can lose hope but not me."

She remembered Roelof and turned. "No! Take you're fingers out of that!" He pulled his hand away from the jar of walnut oil. She kept scolding him, and he snuffed at her, that is, he breathed heavily, back and forth through his nose to hide his anger.

"I'm as tall as that stool," Roelof said, from out of nowhere.

Someone knocked at the back door of the shop, and Clara jumped. If it was Mr. Liebens, he was early. She called through the door; it *was* Liebens. She pulled up the latch.

Even before he got through the door, she demanded, "Tell me about my father."

"In time, in time," he said, breathing heavily.

"What do you mean?" she said. "You're talking about my father. Is he alive?"

"Very much," he said and slowly took a seat on one of the stools. The horse ride had made him sore.

"Why the whispers and secrets? I don't like it." Her face was close to his, but he wouldn't look her in the eye.

"These are delicate matters. Perhaps you are too young to understand, after all." He paused and wiped his forehead. "Yes, I think so. I will go elsewhere." He started to rise.

Clara kept him down with two fingers on his chest. "No, sir, you need to tell me now."

"You know, your father is one of my dearest friends," he said. Clara didn't know that. "But he may be in some trouble."

"What trouble? Speak faster," she said.

He put his hand to his chest, as if to calm his heart. "Oh, you are a very impatient girl," he said. "I have a letter from your father." He pulled an envelope from his jacket pocket and waved it in the air.

"Give it to me!" she said.

On the other side of the room, Roelof was repeating his version of their words like an echo. "Speak faster. Impatient girl," he said to a book.

Mr. Liebens looked from Roelof to Clara. "The letter tells where your father is, but I need something from you before I can give it to you. I'm sure your father would want you to help me." He smiled to reassure her.

"What does he want me to do?" she asked.

"Well, it's not, well . . . I need," he looked into her eyes. "He needs the formula for Battista crimson."

"Okay," she said. Then she remembered. "No, I can't. It's hidden. I don't know where it is. Give me the letter."

He sighed. "I need the color recipe before I can give you the letter."

"I don't understand," she said. "Wait, wait." She backed up a bit. "If my father wanted you to have the recipe, he would have told you where to find it. No. I won't do it. That's a secret color. I won't give it to you." She walked away in a circle, her hands in her hair. Mr. Liebens sat up straight. His eyes lost all their smile.

"No games," he whispered. "Do you want to know where your father is?" Her eyes said yes. "Then find me that color. No color, no letter." He put the letter back in his jacket and struggled his way off the stool. Clara stood in silence, her little finger in the corner of her mouth. *I don't want any part of this. Momma will be furious.* Clara decided to go upstairs to tell Mother everything.

"And don't," Liebens said, "tell anyone about this meeting."

"Why not? I can't do this on my own!"

"If anyone else finds out," he said, putting on his hat, "I will say it is one of your crazy stories, and then I will burn this letter. You will never find your father." With that, he left. She sat down on the hard floor and hid her face in her skirt.

"Crazy stories," said Roelof. Clara looked up at him. He was fingerpainting stripes of orange across his forehead and nose. He growled and said, "Tiger."

# CHAPTER THREE

# Short Cuts

Without looking, Mother could feel the cold from the thin spring snow outside. It was a very late snow, one of those which dusted an already blossoming spring. When Mother came downstairs that morning, she peered through the morning gray at an odd bundle of dirty clothes at the head of the dining table. Mrs. Zoelen snapped her head a smidge at the very thought of such a pile in her dining room, but when she reached to bustle it away, it moved. The pile was Clara. She sat in the head chair, slumped onto the table into her arms, her cape covering her head.

As some sort of defense, Mother squeaked. The cape rose slowly from the table. Then it slid back down. Mother reached over and pulled it off, accidentally snagging some strands of Clara's hair. Clara gave a sharp shout.

"Did you sleep here all night?" Mother asked, arms folded. Clara rubbed her head and pushed the hair out of her eyes. When she saw it was her mother, she stood up quickly.

"I think I slept here all night," said Clara through a yawn.

"Now why would you do such a foolish thing? You have table seams on your cheek." Mother pulled Clara's head to her breast and rubbed the pink seam lines. Clara started weeping muffled sounds into Mother's chest.

Mother held her for a long while and didn't ask for answers. After a few moments, she shuffled Clara into the kitchen, still embracing her.

When they were close to the pantry shelf, Mother reached up and pulled down a brass pastry box. Clara knew the sound the box lid made, and she lifted her head to receive a pastry to help her tears go away. Clara held out her hand to receive it. Mother looked very surprised. "Oh, did you want a pastry? This was for *me*." She smiled and put a delicious piece into her own mouth.

A smile flashed onto Clara's face. "Don't tease, Mother," she said. Clara held out her hand again, and Mother put another bit of pastry into her own mouth. Clara started reaching for the box, willing to wrestle for it, when Mother suddenly popped a bit into Clara's open mouth. Clara instantly doubled over and started hacking and coughing.

Mother let out an "oh dear" and leaned over her, patting her daughter's back, trying to help. Just when Mother started to move toward panic, Clara straightened up, all smiles, no coughs. "Teaser's justice," said Clara. Mother slapped Clara's back very hard.

"So tell me," said Mother, as she leaned against a counter, "why did you spend the night at the table?— as if I didn't know." Clara pointed at her full mouth to explain why she couldn't answer immediately.

"Ahh, food in your mouth never stopped you from talking before. Why now?" Clara nodded, pointing at her chewing again. It was very slow. Mother rolled her eyes, then talked away from Clara. "Your tears are always for your father," she said.

Clara dropped her gaze to the floor and put more pastry into her mouth. Mother sighed a soft string of

*Clara, Clara, Clara.* "What am I going to do with you?" Clara walked over, turned, and leaned back into her mother. "You can't go your whole life waiting for your father. At some point, you have to live around it."

"You mean give up hope," said Clara.

"Yes. Why is that such a bad thing? At some point, yes, you *have* to give up hope."

"But Abraham never gave up hope," said Clara.

"He had a special promise," Mother said, as if from a script she had memorized long ago. "But Ruth's husband never came back. She moved on." Clara put on her I-can't-do-that face.

After a long silence, Clara asked in a new voice, "If someone offered you his house for a special tulip bulb, would it be bad to trade?"

"I don't know," said Mother. "It would depend on the house."

"And what if someone asked you to destroy your best painting to save the life of your favorite horse?" asked Clara.

Mother moved away, uninterested. "Where do these crazy questions come from?"

Clara asked, "And what if someone asked you to keep a secret or else someone special would die?"

Mother sighed as she tinkered around the cutting board. "I guess we've finished our usual chat?" Clara stood waiting for an answer to the last question. "Oh, I don't know. I guess I would keep the secret," said Mother. Clara left the room.

When Mother turned around her insides jolted. Ernst now stood where Clara had been. It seemed like magic.

"May I have some pastry too?" he said.

•   •   •

Out back in the color studio, Clara sifted through stacks of her father's notes. She skimmed through his color-recipe books, staring closely at his margin notes for hints. No Battista crimson. He had showed her some parts of his recipe code. The characters looked something like Hebrew letters but tilted at odd angles with each character surrounded by a circle or a triangle. She peered behind the bookshelves and pushed on panels. She checked for code under the chairs and shelves. But nothing. Father had probably buried it outside or broken up the recipe into five or six books. She didn't even know where to start.

Clara was the first one to get to the school studio that day, and she watched the slow feet of Uncle Caspar coming down the stairs, clump by clump. She turned back to her sketch just before his face appeared. She knew it was too early for him to talk, so she just smiled when their eyes finally met. Still tying his shirt, he rounded his eyebrows at her in return. She was trying to sketch the horse she had ridden from Amsterdam with Ernst. She imagined the shadows along its legs.

Uncle Caspar fiddled with plaster pieces on the other side of the studio. When she thought he was awake enough, she asked softly, "Where did my father keep his most secret color recipes?"

"Please, not so loudly, child!" he shouted. She went back to sketching and waited for the question to settle in his head. After a few minutes, he broke the silence. "He never told us! He wrote them in special code. Hid from his own brothers. Can you believe that? His own *brothers!*"

Uncle Hendrick had entered from the front door during Uncle Caspar's complaint. "Hid them from us, didn't he, Hendrick?"

"Quite true," said Uncle Hendrick, dusting off weak traces of snow. "But I suppose that was because of the Pieter de Hooch mistake." Uncle Caspar puffed out his cheeks in response. "You remember," said Uncle Hendrick, "when we forgot that his special Barbari recipe was a secret. We accidentally sold it to Pieter." He looked at Clara. "We just plain forgot."

"Still," said Uncle Caspar, "that was only one secret. We weren't being malicious."

Uncle Hendrick raised and lowered his eyebrows. "But that would seem like a pretty good reason to hide things from us," said Uncle Hendrick.

"Yes, quite so. Well, at least I'm not bitter against him anyway," said Uncle Caspar.

Clara stopped sketching. "Do either of you know how to mix a Battista crimson?" Both men laughed hard together, then abruptly stopped. They didn't answer her; they just went about their business.

"Truly, though," she said. Both men forced laughter again as they left the room into the back. Clara stopped sketching; her shoulders drooped. Uncle Hendrick returned to the room. As he crossed in front of her, he whispered something. She couldn't make it out.

She mouthed a "what?" He walked back by her, whispering a line of "s" and "oo" sounds. She didn't understand. He came back again and handed her a note. She unfolded it and read "Battista crimson can only be seen in the Soomerschoon tulip." Her forehead grew hot. She started to ask him a question, but he silenced her.

Uncle Caspar came back into the room. "You know, Hendrick," he said, "I believe that Battista crimson can only be seen in the stripes of a Soomerschoon. Isn't that right?" Uncle Hendrick's body sagged.

"You always have to kill it, don't you? How did you know that?" asked Uncle Hendrick as he stormed out of the room.

Uncle Caspar looked at Clara. "What did I do?" She laughed and shrugged.

For the whole school day, Clara could only think about her three bulbs from Amsterdam. She had to get home to plant them. One had to be a Soomerschoon. This had to be an answer to prayer. But she knew it would take too long if she just let them grow normally. She had to force them. Everyone in Utrecht knew how to force tulips early. But Clara needed them to grow faster than usual.

After school, she walked as quickly as possible through the thin snow on the street to her house. She searched all over her room for the three bulbs and finally found them in the pocket of the apron she had worn in Amsterdam. She clomped downstairs and out to the rear garden.

Their little garden area wasn't much bigger than their dining room. You couldn't play out there, but you could sit on the bench and meditate, surrounded by the fence and flowers in the summer. But now everything was brown and white, soil and snow. Clara propped her foot up on the bench and examined her bulbs. *First, shock them with cold. That usually takes three to four weeks. Don't have that sort of time.*

As she thought, she picked up a small flower bowl, emptied the soil and filled the bottom with snow. She carefully set the three bulbs inside and then added more snow, packing it tightly over the bulbs. *Hmmm. What is the coldest part of the garden?* She looked around. *Up high. On the fence. But what if someone knocked them down? I'll wait and watch. Move them at night.* She stood on the bench and stretched in order to set the bulbs on top of the fence.

"Be shocked," she said aloud. *What next,* she thought. *After shocking, take them out of snow. Set them in my room in a bowl of warm water. Better near the fire downstairs. Four weeks, maybe two, I'll have my Soomerschoon. Got to tell Liebens.* She couldn't leave the bulbs up on the fence while she was away, so she climbed back up, grabbed the bulb bowl, and set it down in the corner of the garden. *Put you up when I get back.*

She found Mr. Liebens not far from home. He sat in a nearby town square with his friends. When he saw her he lost his smile and went over to her.

He pretended he wasn't talking to her. He looked around and tried not to move his lips. "Drop the recipe on the ground, and I'll put your father's letter on that low wall over there," he said.

"I don't have it yet," said Clara.

He stared at her, searching her face. "I've got plenty of time. But your father, I don't know." He shook his head.

"I just came to tell you that I've changed my mind. I will do it," she said.

"I had no doubt, no doubt." He straightened his body and laughed. "No doubt," he kept saying.

"It might take me weeks to find," she said. "I can't find it in any of his notes."

"That's too long," he said under his breath as he walked away.

♦   ♦   ♦

When Clara got back home, she put the bowl of bulbs back up on the fence to catch more of the cool breeze. She stood and watched until the evening meal, then she put the bowl back in the corner for the night.

After four days, the snow started to melt away. *Maybe that's a sign,* she thought. *I think they're shocked enough. Come on, boys. Out of the bowl.* She scraped away the snow and pulled out the bulbs. "Shocked, shocked, shocked," she chanted. She warmed some water in a bowl and floated the bulbs in it. She filled another bowl with cold soil and brought it inside to warm up. She let both bowls sit by the fireplace downstairs overnight. Her mother said she was crazy.

The next morning before school, Clara carefully stirred the warm soil and mixed in some rotting vegetable pieces. Into the dark soil she set the three bulbs and covered them. She moved the bowl into her room, and she thought it brought the smell of the country inside. "Grow, grow, grow," she said over them.

A week passed and nothing happened to the bulbs. No shoots, no growth. On some days, her mother would find her yelling at the bulbs, ordering them to behave, to show something.

Two more weeks passed, and although everyone said it was impossible, two of her bulbs showed thin shafts of green just breaking the soil. She yelled at them even more and watered them every morning and evening. They sat in her window and grew little by little. But she could no longer stand the wait. It was all too slow. She met with Liebens several times, and he kept pressing her to find the recipe, but not too hard. Something was odd, though. His eyes never really showed anger. Behind his blustering, Liebens seemed to like this extra time.

. . .

One day after class, Clara asked the uncles where in Utrecht she could find someone with a Soomerschoon.

"Hmmm," they said together, leaning back and puffing their pipes.

"I think Van der Ast had one last year," said Uncle Caspar, squinting in thought.

"No, I think he sold it to Moreelse," said Uncle Hendrick.

"Why do you want to see one this time of year anyway? They're all in bulbs, aren't they?" asked Caspar.

"Bulbs can be very pretty, though," mused Hendrick.

"And some people like to eat them, I hear. But moderation in all things," said Caspar.

"But don't be extreme in that," Clara said. "So where does Mr. Van der Ast live?" Somewhere near St. Luke's, they told her. But he hates children, so don't bother him.

She ran home and nearly stumbled upon Ernst who stood just inside the door. "Come with me. I need your help. Go with me to St. Luke's Guild."

He broke free of her grip. "I can't. I'm supposed to watch Miguel." Roelof peeked around the door at them.

"Come on, Miguel. You can come with us," she said.

St. Luke's Guild was the group to which every serious painter belonged, Protestant or Roman Catholic, but most were Protestant. Mr. Van der Ast was sure to be there. St. Luke's building, an old convent, was set about eight blocks away from Clara's house, in the east part of town. They would have to make several turns and pass over the Oudegracht canal, yet it wouldn't take too long.

But after just two blocks, Roelof started to whine.

He wanted to be carried. Clara tried to carry him a bit, but he was like a sack of potatoes on her chest. She carried him about twenty feet before they went down with a thud. They made him walk a little more, but then after a short distance he sat down in the middle of the street.

Clara got the idea that she and Ernst, together, could carry him. Ernst shrugged, and Roelof lay out flat. Clara lifted him from under his arms, and Ernst lifted his feet. The three of them looked like a very old, sad pony. With all eyes staring at them, they did this for another two blocks.

Finally Ernst said, "I can't carry him any farther." He dropped Roelof's feet, and all three of them sat down. "Let's just make him wait here for us."

"Don't be a dumbhead," said Clara, looking around.

"Don't call me dumbhead," said Ernst.

"I'm just telling the truth. You're being a dumbhead. Shouldn't I tell the truth?" she asked.

"Don't call me dumbhead!"

"Then stop being one," she said in a low tone.

He spoke louder. "Mother told you not to call me a dumbhead! So don't call me dumbhead!"

Clara whispered, "Okay, okay, but you're saying it more than I am. Be quiet," she said through clenched teeth.

"Say it," Ernst said.

She asked 'what?' with her hands.

"Say I am not a dumbhead," he said.

"I am not a dumbhead," she said, then under her breath, "but you might be."

"I am not a dumbhead!" he said. She tried to quiet him down again.

Ernst stood up and started shouting. "I am not a

dumbhead!" Then he made his words sound twisted and stretched like a really stupid person's. "I am nawt a doombhead! I em nawt a dawmbhid! I imm nit a dimbhood!" Clara got up and walked away with Roelof, but Ernst followed and hung on her arm, shouting for all the people around to hear, "I am not a dumbhead!"

"I don't know this boy," Clara kept saying to people who passed by. Soon Roelof joined in on her other arm, and it turned into "We are not dumbheads, wee arr nawt dawmhids!" and so on for two more blocks. Clara was very red when they arrived at St. Luke's.

Their father had always made them wait outside, but he wasn't there. The little spire loomed over them like a mountain. The boys asked to wait outside. Clara stared at the ground then walked right up to the front door. Some men were exiting at the same moment, and she walked right by them. Their heads turned, and a few words of protest fell broken from their lips and died with their shrugs. A few moments later, a uniformed man came out of St. Luke's pulling Clara by the arm.

"Clara's going to get paddled," said Roelof, then he added, "I'm hungry." The boys watched from across the street as Clara tried to get by the guard twice. He kept pulling her out. The boys' mouths hung open. Finally, she started talking quietly to the guard. He listened for a while and then nodded. He pointed down the street and around the corner.

Clara looked around for Ernst and Roelof, but they were watching from behind a wall. Clara couldn't whistle loudly, so she used her usual signal to the boys—a high pitched, almost sung version of a whistle—"beeee-ooooh-wit!" The boys looked at each other and then ran out. Clara walked quickly down the street, and the boys finally caught up with her.

"What was it like inside?" asked Ernst.

"I didn't really look," she said.

"Come on, tell me."

She spoke in a flat tone. "It had blush colored walls with forest green trim. Paintings lined the walls, beautiful paintings. All the artists stood about in little groups chatting and thinking. It was too wonderful. I might sketch it when I get home."

"Where are we going now?" asked Ernst, with Roelof whining beside him.

"Here," she said and stopped in front of a townhouse. "This is Mr. Van der Ast's place. And I think he has a Soomerschoon."

Roelof stared up at Clara and repeated with authority, "Yes, he has a Soorskin."

"You don't even know what that is," said Ernst. Roelof nodded his head up and down.

"What color is it then?" asked Ernst. "How big is it?"

Roelof spread his hands far apart.

Just then the door opened and a wrinkled woman stuck her head out. "Shoo, please. Don't play here."

"I'm here on business," said Clara. "I don't know these vagabond boys."

"What is your business?" asked the woman, already starting to close the door.

"I need to see the Soomerschoon for my father," she said. The woman started chattering at her and told her to go away. The door closed firmly. Clara stood there and could hear voices inside. The door opened and a tall, pale man leaning on a cane stuck his head out and looked down the street. Then he looked down at the children, surprised. He smiled at Clara and waved her in.

"Are you the one who wants to see my Soomerschoon?"

"Yes, sir," she said.

"What are you waiting for? Come on in, come in." The boys moved forward too, but Clara held up her hand behind her back and signaled them to wait.

Roelof looked at Ernst and said, "I'm as tall as the doorknob."

# CHAPTER FOUR

# Pharaoh's Man

Van der Ast's door closed in front of the boys' faces. They looked at each other. Roelof shrugged. But a moment later, the door opened again, and Van der Ast waved them in. Roelof pushed in first.

Clara was staring at one of the many paintings on Van der Ast's wall. Mr. Van der Ast started walking slowly down the hall, his cane being of great use. Clara and the boys followed, and he began to explain the history of tulips. "Their name comes from *toliban*, which is the Persian word for turban, the wrapped coverings the Persians wear around their heads," he told them. "Someone thought that these flowers looked like turbans. So the name stayed." He talked more about their history, and then they all entered a brightly lit room. In the center stood an empty stand. "And here we are," Van der Ast said and swept his arm wide. Clara and the boys looked around, but they didn't see any flowers.

"But sir, where is the Soomerschoon?" Van der Ast's hand was still in the air. He twitched it like a cat's tail, pointing again. The children moved their eyes from the center of the room to the wall, and there hung a painting of the crimson-striped Soomerschoon. It was surrounded by flowers from every growing season. Clara stared at the painting, then looked at Van der Ast, then back at the painting. Her body sagged. Van der Ast read the children's faces.

"Oh, this isn't good," he said. "I see you were expecting the actual flower." He moved his head down to look closer in her eyes. "You look so disappointed. But this isn't even really spring yet. The real Soomerschoon won't bloom for several weeks." He couldn't bring a smile to their faces. "I thought you wanted to see the painting," he said. "I've sold a few of my own, but this was Mr. Bosschaert's. He captured it quite well, I think. Fine *houding.*"

Clara looked at it and shrugged slightly. "Yes, sir," she said. "May I go closer to get a better look?"

"Please, please, young lady. Go forth." The painting stood higher than Clara's head. Van der Ast came over and wanted to lift her up, but his mind was stronger than his body. He called his wife. He explained what he wanted, and she stood firmly behind Clara, gripped her under her arms, and Clara slowly ascended into the air, holding down a giggle. She stared at the image of the Soomerschoon, face-to-blossom. The blossom image was as big as her head, and she wanted to touch it, but she knew better. She leaned her head toward it. Mrs. Van der Ast stifled a breath and shifted her feet.

"What color did the artist use for the crimson?" she asked. Van der Ast stared off in order to remember.

"Bosschaert told me, for I asked the same question," he said. "Now let me see." He rubbed his head with the end of his cane and walked in a bit of a circle. "You know, it's not just *any* crimson. There are about twelve crimsons." He paused, angry with himself. "I just can't remember. But I know who would know, if it's important to you."

"Yes, please," said Clara. She was still dangling in the air.

"Go and see the color merchant, Mr. Nicolaus Zoelen. He knows all such things. The most brilliant color man in Utrecht. I'll find his address for you, but I think he's traveling right now." He started down the hall. Mrs. Van der Ast set Clara down.

"Sir!" Clara cried. Van der Ast stopped. "That's my father." She had come full circle. The day flashed through her mind: lugging Roelof, struggling at St. Luke's, Mr. Liebens always in the back of her mind. And now her journey brought her back to her father's secret. There must be some easier way. She told Mr. Van der Ast a bit about her problem, but not too much. Just before Clara and the boys left the room, Clara asked for one more close look at the color. Mrs. Van der Ast rolled her eyes and lifted her again.

The trip back home took longer than before because Roelof was both tired and hungry. But Clara's mind was already in her father's color shop. She had hit upon an easier way out. She was determined to mix the crimson straight from her memory of Mr. Van der Ast's painting. *I was making this harder than it is,* she thought. *I'm the best color mixer in my class. Seeing the crimson paint itself is actually better than that stupid old flower. Father will be proud. And Liebens gone. Oh, where is Father?*

Clara thought back to the time when she was about seven and had insisted on baking some pastries to sell in the cathedral square, right alongside the other merchants. She was trying to earn money to buy Mother a present. Father sat quietly behind her the whole day, even though it was hopeless. The pastries were a little burnt around the edges, and no one bought a single one. At the end of the day, she hoped Father would just buy them all, but he didn't. Failure was an important lesson. The two of them walked home in the dark, hand in hand, eating all the pastries together.

The next afternoon, in the color shop, Clara gathered as many hints as she could from her father's obvious notes. The first mix was a bit off. It didn't match her memory of the painting. *I should have done this before,* she thought. *I might be with Father now.* She brushed a few streaks on the canvas, then adjusted the mix. She made sure to adjust the written recipe step-by-step. *Memory is a wonderful thing,* she said. *I just needed to see the painting.* She made two more streaks of crimson on the test canvas and smiled. She carried a candle to it, then sat down. *I am a color genius,* she said. *Not me, of course, I had good teachers.*

About an hour passed when she heard a knock. She pictured herself running to the shop door and opening it to reveal Father's beaming face. She opened the door to reveal Mr. Liebens' pumpkin-sized head. He peered into the shop and looked around.

"Yes, I'm alone," said Clara, "and I want the letter now."

"Show me what you have," Liebens said. Clara explained her mixture. She left out the part about Van der Ast's painting. Liebens eyed the crimson-streaked canvas. He picked up her candle and held it close to the sample. Then he pulled something out of his pocket and glanced back and forth between the two. He spotted the recipe sitting on the table below the canvas. He set the candle down on the table and nodded his head.

He smiled with his sausage lips, nodding more. Then he opened his coat and pulled out her father's letter. Clara's cheeks warmed. She wanted to lunge for it. He warmed the letter's wax seal in the candle flame, then opened the seal and removed the letter.

"You must think I'm some sort of fool," he said, and he dipped the corner of the letter in the candle flame. The corner started turning brown, then curling black; a flame jumped from it. Clara shouted and ran toward it. Mr. Liebens held it higher, out of her reach. She grabbed his collar and tried to pull herself higher, jumping, reaching toward the letter. The flames overtook a quarter, then a half, then reached his pinching fingers. He still held on a moment longer, taking the heat into his hand, then dropped the letter. Curls of paper and flame fluttered to the floor. Clara tried to stamp out the flames to save something, but only ashes resulted. She crumpled to the floor.

"Don't play games with me," he said. "Any child can do what you did. Your recipe wasn't even close." He turned. "You've wasted my time; I've wasted your letter. I asked for the master's work, not a child's guesses." He moved to the door. "You have one more chance."

Clara looked up through her tears. "What? Why? The letter is gone." Mr. Liebens pulled and tugged inside his jacket, as if struggling with a mule. He pulled out two more letters.

"There are or were three letters from your father, like three sisters. The first and best sister is now ash. The other two still contain directions to his location. Get me that recipe, or I'll burn these sisters as well." Clara's head sunk to her skirts. When she looked up again, Liebens was gone.

When Clara woke up the next morning, the first thing that came to her mind was that trying to remember the color in Van der Ast's painting had been a pretty stupid idea. She needed the flower itself. She had moved her bulbs out of her room into the garden, where they soaked up the pale, early spring sunshine. She was certain one of them was the Soomerschoon. All three bulbs sat snugly in rich soil. Each had green stems stretching up about the length of a hand. She kept watering them at every hint of dryness and spent long periods of time just sitting and staring at them.

"They won't grow if you stare at them," said Mother, watching from the door.

Clara smiled. "They're getting bigger. I think *this* one is the Soomerschoon."

"Oh Clara, you don't really think that Amsterdam merchant would give one of those away now, do you? They'll say anything these days."

Clara didn't speak, but she knew Mother had to be wrong. The coincidence was just too strong. The exact color she needed "just happened" to be the color in the "mystery" tulip she had bought. She hadn't known that at the time. This was providence, she was sure.

Mother pulled on Clara's sleeve. "Come now, child, we must be off to church." Clara left the pot and followed. The thought of the worship service pulled Clara in two ways these days. She liked confessing her sins with the group, but Mr. Liebens was always there, and the taste of the secret he pushed on her was bitter. It burned at the bottom of her stomach, but she had to be all smiles.

The white arches in their parish church, Buurkerk, reached high and blended with each other in corners, cutting elegant, curved angles in different directions. The highest point of the arches was so tall that Clara imagined that not just one but probably four stacked giraffes could pass under them. Ornate lamps hung down very low throughout the church, but the real lighting came through the stained glass windows; it wandered in among the arches, bouncing off the bone white pillars. The floor was cool slate, and it drew attention to itself because no chairs or pews covered it. People stood for worship.

Roelof, the uncles, and Aunt Griet stood toward the left, with Mother and Ernst on the other side. Mr. Liebens stood at the far back in the crowd of friends called the libertines, people who liked the idea of church but not of creeds. They were known for their grumbling at every sermon and their wild children. Clara could feel Mr. Liebens' eyes on her.

While the pastor was preaching about Pharaoh and the Egyptian midwives, Clara unthinkingly pictured Pharaoh's face as that of Mr. Liebens'. In her mind, she dressed him in much more colorful robes, of course, but it was certainly Liebens there, as the pastor read, "And the King of Egypt spoke to the Hebrew midwives, of which the name of the one was Shiphrah, and the name of the other Puah: And he said, When you do the office of a midwife to the Hebrew women and see them upon the stools, if it be a son, then you shall kill him: but if it be a daughter, then she shall live. But the midwives feared God and did not as the King of Egypt commanded them, but saved the men children alive. And the King of Egypt called for the midwives and said unto them, 'Why have ye done this thing and have saved the men children alive?' And the midwives said unto Pharaoh, 'Because the Hebrew women are not as the Egyptian women; for they are lively, and are delivered before the midwives come in unto them.'"

From high in the pulpit, the pastor explained that just as the serpent had lied to Eve, now it was the daughters of Eve who lied to the serpent—Pharaoh. Serpents don't deserve truth. The serpent's lie had brought curses upon Eve's children, destroying them, but now the midwives' deception protected the Hebrew boys, and God would destroy Pharaoh.

At the end of the worship service, while several hundred members were all slowly filing out, Clara passed by Mr. Liebens. He was holding the hand of a girl Clara's age. Clara and Liebens' eyes met for a brief moment then quickly turned away. They acted like perfect strangers. Clara's mouth was still, but in her head, she shouted *Pharaoh! Pharaoh!*

Just behind Clara, Uncle Caspar reached out his hand to greet Mr. Liebens. Clara slowed down but didn't turn. She tried to listen over her shoulder.

"Good to see you, Liebens! So many folks here; I've only seen you from afar lately. Been working hard with those students, eh?" Uncle Caspar greeted the girl beside Liebens with a smile.

Liebens smiled and patted Uncle Caspar's back. "Yes, yes, been working hard, getting ready for the grand competition."

Uncle Hendrick walked over to Caspar and Liebens. "Yes, Liebens, Caspar and I were admiring some of your students' work on display," he said. "Certainly they will be future Caravaggisti. Hints of great *houding* ahead. We were a little envious, to say the least. They'll certainly be a challenge at the competition." Clara stood a few steps away watching, saying the word *Caravaggisti* in her head. It described what she wanted to be, someone painting in the tradition of Caravaggio, painting that delighted in stark shadows and light, a style all the rage in Utrecht.

"Well, I try . . . We try our best." Mr. Liebens blushed a bit. Clara wanted to roll her eyes. The girl next to

Liebens showed her teeth in a smile. Liebens introduced the girl. "This is Margarieta Grotius, one of my prize painters at the orphanage." The girl curtseyed, and her voice seemed to ooze sugary syrup over everyone.

"Clara," called Uncle Caspar, "Do you remember Mr. Liebens?" Clara smiled and dipped her chin. "Mr. Liebens oversees the orphanage and teaches some of the children there how to paint."

Clara stepped forward a little. "What a marvelous work, sir. What a blessing you must be to them. What a servant."

Mr. Liebens shook his head and kept smiling. "No, no praise. I learn more from them than they from me. They're good children. Just very sad. They delight in painting, like Margarieta here. She came to us from some Franciscan friars over in Arnhem." Liebens looked back at the uncles. "Where is your brother these days? I haven't seen him. I'd love to have him come speak about color at the orphanage."

Uncle Hendrick lost his smile. "I'm afraid he hasn't yet returned from a trip to Venice. We're praying for the best." The chat faded, and they said their farewells.

Uncle Caspar turned to Uncle Hendrick. "I bet he would make a grand deacon here."

Uncle Hendrick nodded, staring off after Liebens. "He's a great fellow. The children adore him. I'd love to go watch him work with those children sometime," said Hendrick. "Quite a talent himself with the brush too."

Clara turned without a word and walked toward the door. She grunted when she passed Mother, Mr. Liebens, and Margarieta talking and laughing. Clara had to get outside; the walls were starting to spin. She told Ernst she was going to run on home.

When everyone else got home, Mother found Clara in the garden again. Clara sat there and lightly scraped what looked like pale dirt from the tulip stems. *Father would put that Liebens in his place. Orphans dorphans,* she thought. But the next morning that same "pale dirt" was back on the tulips. Clara carefully scraped it off again. It was even thicker the next morning. She told herself it was nothing, but she knew. She pretended the tulip stems were straight, but they weren't. She called for Mother to come out, who confirmed that, yes, some plant sickness had attached itself to her tulips. That "dirt" was some sort of mold.

"Perhaps it was too much water and not enough sunshine," Mother said. "Forcing tulips is a delicate business." Mother left Clara alone in the garden. Clara got up and sat on the cold stone bench. *This was my last hope. Now they're dying. First the Van der Ast painting, now no Soomer of my own. I need help. I'll never see Father.*

The next day, after school, Clara waited and fiddled around in the uncles' studio until all the boys had left, including Ernst. The uncles glanced at each other once or twice, then Uncle Hendrick asked, "Shouldn't you be off to bow before your tulips?"

"I need help," she said.

"Oh, I don't feel like bowing before tulips today. Thanks for asking though," Hendrick said. She didn't smile.

"What sort of help?" asked Uncle Caspar.

Clara remembered Mr. Liebens scowling at her and threatening her not to tell anyone about his demand. Then she looked up at the uncles and remembered how they talked about Liebens like he was an apostle. *They will never believe me. Neither will Mother.* She paused.

"I think this is a first," said Hendrick to Caspar. "She can't speak. Write this date down." Caspar stared at Clara.

"What sort of help?" Uncle Caspar asked again.

"I need to break a promise, but I worry about Jephthah," she said.

"Jeph-who?" asked Uncle Hendrick. Uncle Caspar nudged him in the ribs. "Oh, *the* Jephthah in the Book of Judges. Don't worry, he's dead. He won't care."

Clara ignored Hendrick and spoke to Caspar. "Jephthah made a rash promise about killing his daughter, and he still had to keep it. I need you two to help me, but I'm not supposed to tell."

Uncle Hendrick chimed in again. "Please don't tell me if it means you have to kill me. I'm supposed to take Aunt Griet out tonight. She'll be so disappointed."

"Jephthah didn't kill his daughter," said Uncle Caspar.

"Sure he did," said Clara. "He promised God that if he won the battle, he'd sacrifice whatever came out of his house when he got home. And his daughter—"

Uncle Caspar laughed lightly. "He didn't kill her; he dedicated her to service. She couldn't marry, something like a nun. But he certainly didn't kill her. He couldn't promise to do an abomination. God doesn't allow that. If I promised to kill, say, Uncle Hendrick, here, I'm not bound to it. I can't be under oath to sin."

"A good thing too," said Uncle Hendrick. "I say, what would we do without me?" Some door opened in Clara's thinking. She sat up and started speaking quickly.

"So if someone made me promise to keep a secret or else someone would die then, I don't have to keep it?"

"Of course not," said Uncle Caspar. "But you still might have to be very careful. Has someone done this to you?"

"It has something to do with those stupid tulips, I'll bet," said Uncle Hendrick.

"Look, I won't tell you who it is, because you won't believe me. But we don't have much time. It's about Father. He's alive, and this man has asked for Father's secret Battista crimson recipe in exchange for telling Father's location." She spilled the whole story to the uncles, everything except for the name of the person—how she had searched Father's notes, how she had gone to St. Luke's and Van der Ast's, how she had tried to mix the color from memory, how the man had burned the letter. With each sentence out of her mouth, she felt lighter and lighter. "So will you help me?" she asked.

"That can't be a real question," said Uncle Hendrick. "Nothing could keep us away. What a despicable man."

Uncle Caspar paced the room, rubbing his forehead. "First, let us search your Father's recipes again," he said. "Clara, you help me. Hendrick, go find a real Soomerschoon to borrow. Move, move, move!"

# CHAPTER FIVE

# Running Bombs

The uncles canceled school for the next two days, but they didn't explain why. They told Mother it was for a higher good. Uncle Caspar and Clara were in her father's color studio sifting papers once again. Uncle Hendrick was out and about town hunting for the tulip.

At the end of the first day, Uncle Hendrick came knocking on the studio door. Clara ran to open it. She glanced at his hands. Nothing. She walked away without a word.

"Some greeting that is," he said.

"Sorry, Uncle. I wasn't thinking."

He had been all over town. No one knew of anyone having a Soomerschoon.

"Several people told me that the orphanage might have one, a gift from some donor," he said. Clara froze. "So I walked all the way over there. But nothing." Clara tried to breathe normally. "Liebens said he hadn't seen one in years," he added.

Clara snapped around. "Mr. Liebens? You spoke to Mr. Liebens?" Her face was pale behind her forced smile. Uncle Hendrick wasn't looking at her. He was turning pages in a recipe book.

"He was no help," he mumbled.

"I have to go," she said, and she ran out the door. Clara ran down the street, hoping to find Liebens in the square. She crossed street after street, breathing hard, gripping her skirts. *Now all is done. Why didn't I tell them it was Liebens? He's probably already burned the letters!*

She arrived at the place in the square where Liebens often sat. He wasn't there. She spun around, checking every part of the square. Nothing. She ran down a connecting street to the orphanage. He wasn't there, either. Back to the square. Nothing. Her legs were so tired, and her dress was wet with perspiration.

She started back toward home, arms crossed, steps slow. She looked up at the clouds passing in front of the sun for a few steps, then felt a small thump on her back. She turned to look for boys and pebbles. She returned to walking and after a moment felt something hit her again. She scowled and turned around quickly. This time she caught the shape of Mr. Liebens out of the corner of her eye. She looked right at him. He pulled back down an alley. She looked around and walked toward the passageway. When she got there, he motioned her over.

"Your uncle came to visit me," he said.

"But . . . well . . . he doesn't—" she started.

"Have you spoken to them?" he asked.

"No, yes, I mean . . . it was an accident. I didn't—"

"You made me a promise," he said.

"It was an accident. I didn't tell them your name."

He tried to read her face. "I think I'd better burn those letters," he said. "Again, I ask. Did you talk to your uncles?"

Clara took a deep breath and tightened her face. "Because the Hebrew women are not as the Egyptian women."

"What?" Liebens asked. "What are you talking about?"

She answered with that flat, memorized tone of voice, "For they are lively, and are delivered before the midwives come in unto them."

"Stop playing games. Explain." he said.

She closed her eyes and spoke more forcefully, "Because the Hebrew women are not as the Egyptian women."

"I'm leaving," he said.

Clara grabbed his sleeve. "You touch those letters, and you'll get no recipe. I'm close."

"How close?" he asked.

She turned and started walking away. "Close," she said and was gone.

Mr. Liebens stood there with his hands on his hips. A smile barely showed across his face.

When Clara returned home, Mother stood at the door talking to a man who held two paintings, each draped in cloth. He thanked Mother and walked off. Mother waited for the man to be far enough away before she looked at Clara.

Too quietly, Clara asked, "Were those more of our paintings?"

"Yes, Clara. Now, I don't want you pouting about it again. We won't go begging. Selling paintings is the means we have to pay what we owe."

"Did you sell the Moreelse yet?" asked Clara.

"No, not yet. But I am going to have to at some point. Today I sold the Munniks and the Bijlert."

"Not the Honthorst?"

"Please, Clara, don't make it harder than it is." Mother was trying not to think about it. "That was a wedding gift. I've enjoyed it longer than you."

When Clara got to the color studio, she found the

uncles had gone. Roelof was sitting on a stool in the middle of the room with a note stuck to him. He was sitting up too high to get down by himself. Clara removed the note from his shirt, and he watched her eyes as she read. The uncles had written: *Gone to Nieuwegracht dock. New barge arrived with blossomed flowers. May have three Soomerschoons. Bring Roelof and follow.*

Clara folded the note and looked at Roelof. "Can you run fast today?" He shook his head just once. "Well, climb on then, Harry."

"I'm not Harry. I'm Roelof."

"Nope. Today you are *Harry*. It's my job to name you, and today it's *Harry*, or you can just stay trapped on this stool."

In a few moments, Clara, with Roelof on her back, was skipping elephant-like down the street. As they went, Clara proceeded to explain that other names change like his does. She said he was just too young to understand.

"Some names are just too ugly to say," she said. "And other things get tired of their names. Do you see that?" She pointed to a bread shop. "What do they make there?" she asked.

"Bread," said Roelof.

"No, no. See? That's just what I mean. Last week the name changed to *meat*. So when you see bread be sure to call it *meat* now. And there, what's that?"

"I'm hungry," said Roelof.

"No food now. What's that?" she asked.

Roelof looked. "Water fountain," he said.

"No again. You really must keep up with the times, Harry. That's now called a *fire pot*. See how it sparkles in the sunshine? It's a kind of fire. Water we now call

*wine,* and wine is *cake.* But don't you worry. I'll help
you out. You're new to this world."

Clara had to stop and straighten her back. Roelof
slid down onto the street, and she stretched in the sunshine. Roelof stared at the fountain like he had never
seen it before.

"Enough rest? Yes, let's go get that *bomb,*" she said.
Roelof's face lit up as he climbed on.

"Soldiers use bombs," he said.

"No, no, silly boy, that's the old word. I'm speaking about what we used to call *tulips.* Now we call them
*bombs.*" She waited for his reply. He was silent. "Think
about it. Don't tulips look like little explosions?" She
answered for him. "Yes, they do. That's why we now
call them *bombs.* This name-changing thing all makes
sense if you just think about it."

After going several more blocks, they finally came to
the fat, stone bridge that overlooked the canal where
the flower barge sat. The deck looked like a multi-
colored checkerboard; people scurried all over it like
ants. Clara searched the deck for the uncles. She spotted them in front of a maroon square of tulips, and she
called out. They couldn't hear her among all the voices.
Clara set Roelof down, and they held hands and ran
around the bridge, down the steps. They twisted
through the crowd and headed to where she had last
seen the uncles. They were still there.

Roelof turned his head left and right, looking at all
the tulips, "*Bombs, bombs, bombs*, red *bombs*, yellow
*bombs*, purple *bombs*," he said.

Uncle Hendrick was arguing with a flower seller.
"No, I tell you these aren't the same color. We need
that one." He pointed to the crimson-streaked, white

tulip in the bowl held by the merchant.

Clara and Roelof came over and stood beside Uncle Caspar. His face brightened at them, and he bent down to explain what was going on. "The barge had three Soomers, but before we got here, they had already sold two. Now he's saying that this last one is saved for a special person. He says that the crimson of these common Turkish Runcs is the same as that in the Soomerschoon." Clara stared at the live Soomerschoon as it lightly swayed in its bowl. She moved closer. The crimson was very different from that of the painting after all.

Uncle Hendrick's voice grew louder. "Look, name your price for that Soomer! I just have to have it. I'll take full responsibility for explaining it to the person who ordered it. Tell me who it is. He will understand better than you. Now, name your price!"

The short man beckoned Uncle Hendrick to bring his ear down low so he could whisper a price. Uncle Hendrick listened, then snapped up straight. "That is obscene! That is sickening! After all, this flower will die!"

The man waved his hand, brushing Uncle Hendrick off. "You said name my price. I did. That's what the other person is paying, plus the cost of me getting yelled at for selling it to you. Now, if you can't play, then don't waste my time!"

Uncle Hendrick blustered at the man, then shouted out a price that he thought would stop the man in his tracks. Then Uncle Hendrick stood smiling and nodding like he'd won a prize. The man waved him away. Uncle Hendrick thought the man was bluffing, so he started walking away.

"Watch me!" said Hendrick, "I'm walking away.

You're losing money. Watch me." The man waved like Hendrick was a child, then turned to other customers.

"Ooh, you're a monster. You sure showed him," said Uncle Caspar. Hendrick elbowed him in the ribs.

"But that flower is in his hands," said Clara, her eyes becoming moist. "My father—"

Uncle Caspar frowned at Hendrick. "We just have to wait for the buyer. We can't leave."

"I'm not going anywhere," said Uncle Hendrick. "My eyes will not leave that pot." The four of them sat down on the edge of the barge and waited. An hour passed, then two. The tulip merchant finally made them get off of his barge and wait on the dock. There they waited, surrounded by crowds of tulip buyers.

Clara spied a very determined blond boy making his way through the crowd. He found the main merchant and handed him a note.

"That must be it," said Uncle Hendrick. Caspar was already walking. The boy handed the flower merchant a long pouch, and the man handed him the bowl with the Soomerschoon. Clara stayed on the dock with Roelof, but when the trade was made she noticed that more than just her uncles moved. Several small groups of people made their way through the crowd to the boy, who was now carrying the Soomerschoon close to his chest.

People tried to stop him, and he started to yell as it became more difficult to walk. "My master said not to stop or talk. Please let me through. Got to go!" As he left the barge for the dock, he passed right by Clara, and she started speaking quickly. He kept walking and ignored her.

"I don't want your stupid tulip! I just have to borrow it, or my father will be lost!" The boy kept moving. "Please help me!" But he didn't stop. Clara stamped her foot.

Roelof looked up at her like she had really confused things. "You said *tulip* not *bomb.* You should have said *bomb.*"

The uncles and a half-dozen other men followed the boy closely. "Stop following me!" the servant cried. "My master will be angry."

Some of the men called out, "Who is your master?" and other things. When the boy got to the top of the steps, many were still close on his tail, so he started to jog, then they jogged after him, then he started to run, and they ran too, with Uncle Hendrick in the lead. From the dock, Clara and Roelof could see the train of people moving quickly after the boy as he headed up toward the highest part of the bridge's arch.

Uncle Hendrick was shouting, "I just want to talk to you, boy!" But the boy ran faster, and Uncle Hendrick's long legs couldn't keep up. The boy just about vanished over the arch of the bridge when everyone heard the boy shout, as if in pain. He had tripped himself on the cobblestone.

Immediately everything went silent as all eyes watched the pot and Soomerschoon fly through the air, more slowly than it really flew. It landed on the edge of the bridge. The crowd gasped. And it started to roll, first for a flick of a moment back toward the street, then toward the canal, and off it tumbled. Uncle Hendrick  and everyone lunged for the side of the bridge.

Clara sat open-mouthed as she saw the bowl spewing dirt and snapping the Soomerschoon around, tumbling end over end toward the water. She closed her eyes so hard it hurt and waited for the splash. When it came, she opened her eyes, just in time to see Uncle Hendrick standing on the edge of the bridge, stripping off his outer jacket, with Uncle Caspar grasping uselessly after him. Hendrick jumped—not a dive—just a sort of shot-bird drop into the canal. He vanished beneath the spray of waves for a moment, but when he came back up, he was spluttering and spitting. His hands were empty. He smacked at the water, but the flower was gone. The bowl had dragged the Soomerschoon to the bottom of the canal. After Uncle Hendrick was pulled from the water, he didn't stop fussing and arguing, most of all with himself. Uncle Caspar just let him go on and on.

They had made their way through the city streets, with Uncle Caspar carrying Roelof on his back. His father, Uncle Hendrick, was still too wet. His shoes and clothes made sloshing, sucking sounds all the way home.

"So, *now* what do we do?" asked Clara.

Uncle Hendrick jumped right in. "I say we move from this horrible city. What has it come to? Chasing boys for flowers. It's all nonsense I say. What a despicable place. I hate tulips."

"Bombs!" said Roelof and looked at Clara. She nodded approval.

"Excuse me, Uncle 'Swan Dive,' but you were one of those people chasing the flower," said Caspar.

"I really hadn't forgotten, dear brother. Really hadn't. But I wasn't lusting over the flower like those riff-raff running behind me. I just wanted to borrow it for the color of its veins. Is that so unreasonable?" They had already been through this discussion three or four times on the walk.

Clara spoke again, more to Uncle Caspar. "Truly, though, what shall we do?"

"I think we'll have to start searching the city for those other two Soomerschoons," Caspar said. Uncle Hendrick groaned.

"That could take forever," said Clara.

"And after the report of the flying Soomerschoon gets around," said Hendrick, "I'm sure they'll be very well-hidden."

They finally arrived at the uncles' studio door, and they were all dragging tired legs. Clara followed them in, and the four of them sat around a table to rest their feet for a moment. All except Roelof tilted their heads back in their chairs and closed their eyes. "Bomb," mumbled Roelof.

"Why is this so hard?" said Clara slowly.

"Bomb," said Roelof.

"If good color were easy, my dear," Caspar sighed, "your father would never have had to travel all the way to Venice in the first place."

"Bomb," said Roelof.

"Nothing of quality is easy, my dear," said Hendrick. He rubbed the bridge of his nose.

"Bomb," said Roelof more loudly.

"Yes, yes," said Clara to pacify him. "Bomb in the water."

Clara lifted her head and looked at Roelof, and then something on the counter caught her eye. She gasped. Uncle Caspar lifted his head and gasped too.

"I'm so sick of gasps today," said Uncle Hendrick. "Can't anyone just speak or draw me a picture?" All four of them stared at the same spot on the counter. There, amid soiled rags and jars of brushes, sat an exquisite china bowl packed with the finest soil, holding up a long green stem, blossoming at its peak with a real, angelic Soomerschoon tulip—a bright cream background with several wide ribbons of royal crimson climbing each petal.

"Bomb," said Roelof, finally vindicated.

Their mouths hung open, and no one could speak. The uncles instantly got up. Clara ran over and stood before the tulip like it was the burning bush. They all gathered round, but no one got too close.

Uncle Hendrick whispered, "Bomb."

Uncle Caspar whispered, "Bomb."

Clara closed her eyes. It was as if her father stood before her, an answer to all her hopes. Her mind ran on its own, searching for words of gratitude and relief— "What is your only comfort in life and death? That I with body and soul, both in life and death, am not my own. . ."

# CHAPTER SIX

# Staring Deeply

"What is the hurry?" Mother asked. Clara pulled her along the street toward the uncles' studio. Ernst jogged behind them.

"It's a miracle! You have to hurry for miracles," said Clara. They pushed open the door, and the uncles still stood before the Soomerschoon tulip, mouths hanging a little open. Roelof stood on a rickety stool on the other side of the room. He was twirling a small plaster model of a woman around his head. Mother humphed, went over, and pulled him off the stool.

"I'm hungry," Roelof said.

Clara beckoned Mother over as if the flower were about to vanish. The uncles and Ernst reluctantly cleared out of the way for Mother to see. She stared at the tulip for a moment as the others stared at her face, waiting for the smile.

"Very nice," she said as if merely judging a good tomato; she turned toward the door.

"*Very nice?*" repeated Uncle Caspar.

"They all look the same to me," Mother shrugged. "Where did it come from?"

"That's just it," said Clara. "It just showed up here. We don't know who put it there."

Ernst frowned. "Maybe it got lost." Mother rolled her eyes a bit. "Or an angel brought it," he said. Clara smacked his head.

Mother said, "I think I heard talk that those stripes come from some bug."

"Then it's a glorious bug," said Clara. They all stared at the cream and crimson tulip, glowing amidst its three green leaves. Mother left, and the others kept staring.

After a moment, Clara broke away from the frozen group and started rummaging through the color supplies. She would need the powders that created paint colors once they were mixed with linseed oil. Many of the powders, like yellow ochre and white lead, had been ground from naturally-colored plants and minerals. She carried what she needed over to a mixing table and set down a crusty cup of linseed oil, several dry, yellow ochres, and some minium powder.

"Where is the white lead?" she asked over her shoulder. The uncles quickly looked at each other, then walked over and started putting away the very things she had just brought out.

"What are you doing, sirs?" she asked. "I'm using those." They kept putting things away.

"We've got the flower," she said. "I'm going to mix its crimson and find my father. Please stop." They didn't.

"What do you think you're doing?" Uncle Caspar asked. Clara stood silently with her arms folded.

"You are insulting the Soomerschoon," said Uncle Hendrick. She tilted her head and frowned. "Come here, girl," he said and led her to the flower. "Do you see that color?" She nodded.

"No, you don't," Caspar insisted. "You're looking at it, but you don't see it. You're judging by appearances. If you really saw it, you wouldn't grab old linseed or any of those other ingredients. You must know the color before you can mix it. You have to live it for a while, breathe its color."

She knew where this was going and didn't like it. "No," she whined, "we don't have time. My father may be dying." She stamped her foot

"If you don't do it right, Clara," said Hendrick with an edge in his voice, "he'll burn the next letter." She looked away.

"I don't have time," she pleaded. "What about moderation?" she asked.

"Moderation isn't an excuse for bad work and impatience," said Uncle Caspar.

Uncle Hendrick said, "And I'm pretty sure that moderation in preparing color is a crime in Utrecht."

"Quite so," said Caspar. She made a move back to the ingredients. The uncles blocked her way.

*Patience, patience, that's all I ever hear,* she said to herself.

"You know the routine for fine colors. Only the freshest linseed." His head pointed to the door. "To the farm."

She turned and pulled her hair until it hurt, and then some more. She turned back. "Ernst is coming with me though, not Roelof," she said.

"Uh-oh," said Uncle Hendrick. "This must be a dark day. She called it *Roelof*." Clara grabbed Ernst's hand, and they started off. Uncle Caspar stopped them to give them money for the trek.

When she was gone, the uncles looked at Roelof. He started to speak. Uncle Hendrick held up his hand. "Let me guess. You're hungry." Roelof smiled.

His father picked him up and carried him like a rifle at his waist. Roelof's head and legs hung down. "Time to feed my puppy-boy," Hendrick said and left.

◆　◆　◆

Ernst and Clara skipped along the streets heading toward the west city gate of Utrecht called Katharijnepoort. They crossed the main square—Stadsplaats. Even before they reached the west gate, Ernst started sneezing. As he walked along, he pinched his nose to keep out the spring dust.

When they approached the double-arched bridge leading out of the city, a heavily cloaked man walking toward them from the bridge suddenly bolted to the side and ran down the nearest side street. The hood over his head had cast a shadow over his face. Clara shrugged her shoulders at Ernst and kept walking. They always saw something strange while out in the city.

Once they had crossed the bridge and passed under the second arch, a green, buzzing world of farms snapped into view, as if they had stepped through a magical door. Outside the city lay eternal farmland. They made their way down the wide dirt road and turned right along a row of small farm plots, each with different vegetables and flowers.

The best linseed plants came from the Blau farm. Mr. Blau couldn't speak and didn't smile, but he knew his linseed. His plants produced the clearest oil, perfect for mixing colors. Clara eyed the rows of newly-cut linseed plants like a chef selecting steak cuts. She pulled out the ones she liked and piled them across Ernst's outstretched arms. When she couldn't see Ernst's chin, she knew she had enough. They paid Mr. Blau, and he tipped his hat. As they turned back toward the city, they could see the tall wall wrapping around the city, capped on the northwest stretch with five windmills slowly waving to the farms.

Crossing back into Utrecht, Clara noticed that same strangely-cloaked man walking a stone's throw in front of them, going the same direction he had been going

before. Ernst was starting to struggle under his bundle
of linseed plants and couldn't see too well. Something
about the man was too familiar. Clara called out to him.
He turned, looked at them and started to run off again.
This time, though, the hood over his head blew off as
he ran, and from the back, the man seemed oddly familiar. *The same thin blond locks. The same-shaped head
. . . as Father!*

Clara called out "Father!" and started running after him. Ernst tried to jog along, but he didn't get very
far before he stopped. The man ran through the square,
and Clara followed closely. He looked back at her and
ran into a man carrying a stack of books. Clara jumped
over the scattered books and followed him up a dark
side street. He turned left, and Clara heard a crash of
boxes. When she got there, she didn't see him at all. A
jumbled pile of wooden crates stood to the side of the
narrow street. One of the boxes teetered and slid down
to the street. On tip-toe, she slowly peered between
slats of wood into the heart of the pile. She pulled a bit
at one of the boxes, but it didn't budge. She pulled
harder, and the whole side of the pile slid toward her
like a waterfall. She jolted back, tripping over her feet,
and landed flat on the street, with a couple of boxes
across her legs. But the man wasn't inside the pile. He
was long gone.

Clara leaned up on her elbows, then pulled her legs
out from under the boxes, just as Ernst came up, breathing hard.

"You called him *Father*," he said between breaths.

"He looked just like him from behind," said Clara.
"He even ran like him."

"But he didn't stop," Ernst said.

"No." She shook the image out of her head, "I must
be seeing things." When they told the uncles about the

cloaked man, the uncles joked that perhaps it was Father playing a very elaborate prank. Clara frowned.

Ernst laid the linseed plants out on a broad table, and the uncles eyed them carefully, setting some to the left and others to the right, sheep and goats, they said. At the back of the studio, the four of them stood by various stone contraptions and mills for squeezing the oil out of the plants. Clara preferred a kind of millstone with a funnel at the bottom. She pressed and squeezed, moving faster and faster, catching more and more drips of oil. Uncle Caspar came over and touched her arm. She looked up in a flurry, strands of hair loose over her eyes.

"You're going to kill the oil," he said quietly.

She smiled. "No really, I'm doing fine." She went back to pressing.

His grip tightened on her arm. "Stop and breathe," he said. "Patience makes the best oil. Do it right or don't do it at all." She sighed and let him show her a better, slower way.

When they had squeezed all the oil they needed, it was very milky, as usual. They still had to purify it so that it would be as clear and thin as water. Clara and Ernst came out of the back room each carrying two clear, pear-shaped bottles. The uncles sat at the mixing table, one sifting white sand, the other sifting salt. They poured the cloudy linseed oil into the four bottles, filling them only halfway. They filled the rest of the space with clean water.

Ernst was put in charge of the salt. He put two handfuls in each bottle, followed by Clara pouring two handfuls of white sand in each. The uncles finished the process by dropping two handfuls of dried bread crumbs into each. With all this, the bottles seemed to contain nasty little storms within. But the salt, sand,

and bread would each do its part to suck impurities to themselves from the oil and settle on the bottom.

"Are we ready to shake?" asked Uncle Hendrick. They each took hold of a bottle and stepped back from each other. Then they started shaking, up and down, side to side. They did this without talking for a while, then set them down and stared. Slowly the water and oil separated.

"So when will it be clean? Tonight?" Clara asked. The uncles looked at each other.

"This is oil, not a pastry pie," said Uncle Hendrick. Clara mumbled a bit and looked down.

"Remember," said Uncle Caspar. "We know oil."

"How long?" she said, not really wanting to hear.

Uncle Caspar breathed in and prepared himself for a storm from Clara. "Beauty takes patience. And we're making beauty." He paused. "Three weeks," he said.

"Oh," she said, looking down. She was still trying to figure out patience. "Is that all?" She turned and quickly walked outside into the street without a word. Even with the front door closed, the uncles and Ernst could hear her scream at the top of her lungs. She came back in, all smiles.

"Well, what's next?" she asked, her smile a little too wide.

Uncle Caspar stepped forward. "Well, we must shake these bottles three times every day and add new bread every few days. Then we'll have to cook it and let it sit in the sun for the last week. Everyone says this time of year has the perfect sun for bleaching, when it's not raining."

"In the meantime," said Uncle Hendrick, "you must do the hard part. Study the tulip. It won't last forever."

"Why just me? Can't we do it together?"

"We never knew colors like your father," said Caspar. "And he couldn't paint to beat a dog," added Hendrick.

"But," said Caspar, "you have your father's blood for seeing color, if you'll only work at it. And you've been with him when he's worked at it. What sort of things would he do?"

Clara didn't answer. She walked over to the tulip as if in a trance. She stood there for quite a while and didn't move. The uncles and Ernst left her alone to stare.

Ernst practiced drawing, then soon became bored. He walked around, fiddling with things, waiting. Then he remembered a trick he had learned. He got in his uncles' line of sight and walked toward the front door. Then he kept walking right into the door, a loud knock clapped out, and he fell to the ground holding his forehead; he moaned. The uncles ran over to help him, lifting him by the arms. They told him to stop that silly crying, but he wasn't crying. He was trying to hold in his laughing.

"I didn't hit my head," Ernst said through giggles. "I got my head close and then kicked the door with my foot just when my head would hit." The uncles pulled him to his feet. They smiled and nodded.

"You mean like *this?*" asked Uncle Hendrick, and he pushed Ernst's head against the door so it really bumped.

"No, brother, let me try. It was more like *this*." Uncle Caspar kicked the bottom of the door and then also bumped Ernst's head into the door again.

"No, no, no, Caspar. The foot and head must hit the door at the same time, like *this*." And he demonstrated again with Ernst's head.

Clara looked over at them. "Do you mind? Artist at work here."

The uncles let Ernst go, and he walked away smiling and rubbing his head. They went back to their various projects. Every now and then they would steal a glance sideways at Clara and see her gently touching the petals, bending them in the light just a bit. After a while, she pulled up a stool and sat down.

About an hour later, she said, "I think I've got it!" Silence. Then she turned around to face them. The uncles groaned.

"Don't even think that's true!" shouted Uncle Caspar. Clara sat silently.

"Your father," said Hendrick, "would never think he had captured a color after just staring at it for two hours."

"I thought that was pretty good," said Clara.

"You thought wrong," said Caspar. The uncles stood tall, right in front of her, staring down.

"Your father took weeks to capture a color. What did he do during that time?"

Clara stared off into her memory, and her body began to sag as she remembered. She remembered him taking colored objects into the sun, into the shade, into church, out to the farms. He held candles in front and behind. He would hold a color close to his eye and look at it across the town square. He would put it next to other shades of the same color, and then against very different colored backgrounds. It all seemed to take forever. She turned and picked the flower bowl up off of the counter and headed out of the studio without a word.

"I hope she knows what she's doing," said Caspar.

"I hope it works," said Hendrick, brushing out an

earthen jar. "I wish there were an easier way."

Ernst's face lit up. "I've got it," he said and clapped his hands. "Why can't we just take the tulip apart, then cut the crimson stripes out, and smash them till they bleed the color we need?"

Uncle Hendrick dropped the jar on the floor, and it smashed. He started walking toward Ernst like a lion hunting its prey. Caspar got in front of Hendrick to slow him down.

"Calm down, brother," Caspar soothed.

"Get that heathen boy out of our studio," said Hendrick through clenched teeth. Ernst had a big grin on his face.

"Just cut it up," Ernst threw out again louder, making knife moves in the air.

Caspar still held Hendrick back. "Let me talk to the monster," said Caspar. Pushing back on Hendrick, Uncle Caspar spoke slowly. "Ernst, my dear savage, it appears you have insulted everything good and holy in this room. I can't hold your Uncle Hendrick back much longer. Would you mind running home and asking your mother to give you a good, solid spanking?"

Ernst walked up to the uncles struggling against each other. "Should I bring a knife back when I'm done?" The uncles screamed and broke apart and snapped their arms at him. He ran for the door, and they stood with their hands on their hips. Just before he opened the door, he did his pretend-to-hit-his-head trick on the door again, falling backward, holding his head.

"We could only wish!" said Uncle Hendrick. Ernst popped up and left, laughing and waving an imaginary knife.

♦   ♦   ♦

For the next two weeks, Clara spent every spare moment in her father's color shop or carrying the Soomerschoon around the house and garden, holding it up, comparing it to anything and everything, in shadows, in sunlight, reflected in water. She was up early; she was up late.

Toward the beginning of the third week she concocted practice-mixes with old oil to start off with. She laughed at herself, remembering what ingredients she had picked up that first day back at the uncles' studio. She still used a bit of crushed yellow ochre and minium, but the two main ingredients were powders called vermillion and Indian lac. She combined these in different quantities, some too dark, some too bright. She tried to think like her father; she tried to think like Jacob working for Rachel in the Old Testament. She tried mixing the powders in walnut oil and then again in linseed oil. Every attempt got closer. But for most of the week she couldn't capture that special brightness of the Soomerschoon crimson. She searched through her father's books again and again, finally stumbling upon his hint that by adding wine to vermillion mixes, one could bring about a very special brightness. She quickly borrowed wine from her mother and went back to mixing and remixing.

She must have mixed different shades of crimson ninety times. She pulled out a blank canvas and started testing stripes of crimson from the different recipes. The uncles came over every few days to check in on her and to pacify Mother about the importance of Clara's mission.

She spent plenty of time in the decipherable parts of her father's notes. The recipes for many small solutions sat there in his notebooks. That was the hardest part. She was giving away tricks and secrets and bits of wisdom he had built together over decades. And here she was copying much of it. But giving these things to Liebens, who would probably give them to the world, would ruin Father's business. His secrets would be gone, and he would be just another color merchant. But she had to give them to get him. How could her father be satisfied without his unique color recipes upon which he'd built his reputation? Yet if she didn't reveal these secrets, would her father come back at all? She didn't know.

As the days wore on, the uncles showed up more frequently. "Are we there yet, Clara?" they would ask. The more they showed up, the greater pleasure she took in reminding them that "Beauty takes patience" and "We want to do it right or not at all, don't we?" The uncles usually grumbled to themselves and said things like, "Don't be extreme in your patience!" and more desperately, "Don't be a patience-monster." But they didn't really mean it.

Back at the uncles' studio the linseed oil had been moved from the bottles, cooked but not boiled, and then set outside in the perfect spring sunlight. The sun removed any leftover water drops. When it had sat outside for a week and a half, being bleached and thinned to a mountain-water clarity, the uncles declared it perfect.

At nearly the same time, Clara sat amid six or seven canvases of crimson stripes and crosses, some on light backgrounds, some on dark. On the night of the end of the third week, she dipped a brush in a mix and laid down a crimson stripe on another canvas crammed with crimson stripes, each ever so slightly different from the previous one. She stared at this shade long and hard, but she knew before she brushed it on that this was the one. A broad smile transformed her face. She made several more test stripes on that canvas, then started a new one. She checked it in her candlelight and then held it outside in the moonlight.

Apart from being a bit too shiny, it was perfect. The new linseed oil might cure the shininess. The oil was the only thing it lacked. She covered the paint jar and made sure she had written down the exact recipe and saluted the weakening Soomerschoon sitting on her father's desk. So many failed crimson recipes lay at her feet. She leaned back in her father's big chair, stretched her arms behind her head, and fell asleep.

The next morning her uncles found her asleep on a floor covered with crimson spatters and recipe notes. She woke with a grin, and they all sped off toward the new linseed oil, not forgetting the tulip. They mixed the paint ingredients and fresh linseed oil together in the uncles' studio. She tested it before showing the uncles, and she thought it still too shiny. The fresh linseed oil hadn't cured that. She explained the shininess problem to the uncles.

"We were waiting to see if you ran into that problem," said Caspar. They were nodding and smiling too much.

"Your father gave us the cure once," said Hendrick. "But he told us it was a deep family secret."

"So if we tell you, you'll have to give us your first-born child." Clara just stood waiting with her hands on her hips.

"Okay," he tried. "You can keep your future child. And I'll trade it for babysitting Roelof."

She was unmoved. "I have to do that anyway," she said.

"She's too bright for you, Hendrick," said Caspar.

"I'll give the secret to you because you are your father's daughter. That's good enough for you. But you must promise never to let it slip out of your lips. Your father would make us bleed."

"We don't like to bleed," added Hendrick. She nodded. Hendrick went over to a shelf and pulled a little bottle of golden oil from the back.

"This is spike oil," he said. "Add just a few drops to reds or blues, and it makes the color sink in without being shiny. The color will keep its brightness too, never fading." She held out her hand. Hendrick pulled his back. He handed it to Caspar who handed it to Clara. It seemed a bit like wizardry, thought Clara. But she took it and added two drops to the jar of Soomerschoon crimson. The uncles told her to be sure not to write it in the recipe for the man.

When the mix was blended better, she painted it onto one of the uncle's canvases and held it up next to the Soomerschoon itself. The uncles saw the actual color now for the first time. They were speechless for once in their lives. They stared for the longest time, far and near, pacing by it, standing still. Pure silence. Clara didn't need them to say anything. She took her written recipe and a big jar of the perfect crimson and headed off to the orphanage through a light rain to find Liebens. The uncles just stood there.

When she had been gone for quite a while, Uncle Caspar broke the silence. "I never thought she had it in her."

Uncle Hendrick said, "It must be in the blood. How could a thirteen-year-old do that?"

Caspar whispered, "Stubborness. Stubborness turned into patience."

"Her tyrant had better like it," said Hendrick.

# CHAPTER SEVEN

# Hungry Spies

Ernst and Roelof pressed themselves inside a doorway, a few houses down from the uncles' studio. The thin and pale sunshine made ghost shapes up the street. Roelof started to talk.

"Shhh," said Ernst. "Spies have to be quiet." Roelof tried to whisper, but he really couldn't, and it came out like slow talking. Ernst put his hand over Roelof's mouth. Roelof licked Ernst's palm. As Ernst kept staring toward the uncles' door, he pulled away his spitty palm from Roelof's mouth and rubbed it off on Roelof's head.

"I'm hungry," said Roelof.

"Shhh, spies don't eat," whispered Ernst. Roelof thought about this, and his face started turning into a tomato, no tears, just every face muscle pulled and pushed.

"I . . . don't . . . want . . . to be a spy." He started snuffing again. "Going . . . to . . . Mother," said Roelof. Just then the uncles' door opened, and out walked a determined Clara. She had a jar of paint in one hand and was tucking a folded paper into her skirts.

"There she is," said Ernst. Roelof forgot all about food and his face instantly went smooth again. They watched her go down the street, and when she turned the corner, the boys followed, darting into doorways and behind wagons. She hadn't seen them, even when she reached the orphanage.

Mr. Liebens was just closing the door at the orphanage when Clara arrived. That sugary girl, Margarieta, was with him.

"I'm sorry," he said in a huff, "We've got to run some errands. I should be back in a few hours."

Clara locked him in a stare. He withered a bit. "Well, run along, girlie. I can't talk now." She didn't move. She just stood in the rain. Margarieta smiled the whole time as if she were at a party. Liebens had never seen Clara stare at him like that, and he fumbled some things in his hands, dropping them. Clara leaned over, careful not to spill the paint, and handed his things back to him.

"Well, I might have just a minute. Come in quickly then. We're getting wet." She slowly followed them down the hall and up the stairs to his office. The rest of the orphanage was gray and bare, but his office walls were full of the most beautiful paintings. It was hard for Clara to keep her eyes on her business with such walls.

They came to his desk, and Clara asked in a flat, steady tone. "Do you have my letter?"

"Should I leave, Mr. Liebens?" asked Margarieta, curtseying deeply and waving her hands like a lost ballerina. She longed to stay and see this Clara girl put in her place. Liebens nodded his head to send Margarieta off. She forced another smile and stopped in front of Clara before she left.

The two girls stood awkwardly for a moment and then Margarieta wrapped her arms around a stiff Clara in a hug. Clara frowned, and Margarieta walked off quickly. Liebens just waited like he'd seen it a hundred times.

"Look," he said to Clara when Margarieta was out of the room. "I have someone else working on the Soomerschoon color, so I don't really need you. I hadn't heard from you for weeks, and that last joke of a mix was quite worthless."

"Do you have my letter?" she asked again.

"Show me the mix," he said. She didn't move. "Yes, I've got the stupid letter right here, but I need to see the paint first."

Clara set the jar of paint on his desk, and he took it over to one of his empty canvases and brushed it on. He stared at it and pulled some samples out of his pocket like the first time. He took the canvas over to the sunlight coming through the window. He set it all down and came back to her.

"Yes, that will do," he said, wiping his hands. "That will do just fine for the competition. We've got to go now. Hand over the recipe." While Clara was getting it, Liebens stepped over to his desk chair and reached into a chocolate-colored coat that hung around it. Out came a letter.

"Show me my father's handwriting first," Clara said before handing over the recipe. Liebens unfolded the letter, whose seal had already been broken, and showed her a folded portion of it. Her heart leaped to see her father's handwriting. They stood silently for a moment, each waiting for the other to hand over the other's paper. Liebens reached out first, perhaps realizing that he could just take the recipe from her if she refused. She took her father's letter and pressed it against her breast and stretched out her hand with the recipe for Battista crimson. Liebens snatched it and turned away, studying it.

Clara still stood there, just clasping the letter to

herself. When Liebens turned back, he looked a little nervous. "You probably won't like your father's letter. But I'm tired of this game. I don't want any further part in it." Clara unfolded the letter and started reading it. Liebens spoke over her silent reading. "You will think I am the bad one, but I'm not."

Clara noticed first that the letter was addressed to her mother. How did Liebens get it? She read down the letter, where her father had written, *I followed the land route back from Venice and took an illness just outside of Paris.* A few lines further, he noted, *I should be home within the month, if all goes well.* She smiled broadly for a moment, then paled.

"When was this written?" she asked.

Liebens was pretending to be busy, shuffling some papers. "Oh, I'm not sure. Does it really matter?" Clara turned the letter over and found a date written by the seal. *The letter was four months old!*

"This letter is useless! It's too old," she said. "Give me the third letter!" Liebens set his hand on the chocolate-colored jacket. He stumbled over his words.

"Look—this—you and I agreed. You worked for a letter, and I gave it to you as promised. No complaints—you can't complain now."

Clara eyed the coat and took a step closer. "Is the third letter more recent?"

"Very recent."

"You're a vile man," said Clara. "You are playing with my father's life." Her face went pink at the edges. With a low, strained voice, she said, "You gave me Leah, not Rachel."

Liebens rubbed his forehead. "It's not at all what you think. I'm not giving the orders here. Please don't hate me," he said. He growled at himself and paced.

"It's not me, you see. I don't really understand it my-self," Liebens said. "It seems awfully cruel—your fa-ther."

"What are you talking about?" Clara asked.

"Oh, I'm in so much trouble if I say." He looked at the ceiling. He still needed her.

"What?" Clara asked.

He blew a breath through his circled lips. "The truth is, *your father put me up to this*. He has actually been in Utrecht for several months now." Clara took a step back. "Look, I just want to work with the orphans," he added. "I don't like tricking children or testing them or doing whatever he's doing to you. But don't be an-gry with me. I love children, and I'm sure you're a nice girl. I would never want to upset you."

"You are a liar," she said slowly. But her mind kept flashing to images of the hooded man.

Liebens' hands hung palms up. He spoke like some-one bearing bad news. "You know how your father likes jokes and tricks."

Clara's face was frozen, except for her nostrils. The silence got too thick. The hooded man again. The let-ter slipped out of her fingers and floated in sails to the floor. She turned and started out of the room.

He was almost in tears for her, but he added, "And if you want the third letter, you still mustn't tell any-one. I have rules to follow. I'll have to burn it." He said this last part as if he were apologizing.

Clara left the house and started off through the rain. Rain drops worked their way through the embroi-dery of her cap and slid down some loose strands of her hair, but she didn't care. She walked slowly, almost wanting to feel the rain against her skin. But she didn't head home. She walked toward the Katharijnepoort gate to look for the man in the hooded cloak.

◆   ◆   ◆

When Clara wandered out of the orphanage, Ernst and Roelof pulled back behind a wagon down the street. They didn't really care what she was doing or where she was going. They just wanted to spy and not get caught.

"I'm hungry," said Roelof.

"Stop it. Will you just stop it!" whispered Ernst. "I don't want to hear any more about you being hungry. You should have finished your meal this morning. But you didn't. We've got to follow her."

Roelof looked at him like a beggar and did some more snuffing.

Ernst had to stop Roelof's crying, somehow. He rubbed the rain off Roelof's forehead. He took on a bright face and kneeled down to Roelof's level. "Look, you're young, but *hungry* doesn't mean what it used to. I got mad at you because I thought you were saying something else. Nowadays, when anyone says *I'm hungry* that's how they greet someone on the street. Instead of saying, *hello* or *good day, sir,* we say *I'm hungry* and pat our heads. Like this. So that's why I got mad just now. I forgot you didn't know that, and I thought you were just saying *hello, hello, hello, hello* over and over again. Get it?"

Roelof nodded. "But I *am* hungry."

"Now, if you are really hungry in the old way, we don't say *I'm hungry* anymore. We say *I'm a dumbhead.*"

"Noooo," said Roelof, chuckling.

"True, true," said Ernst. "Food goes into your head, and *dumb* means empty. So if you need food, you say my head is empty. Or *I'm a dumbhead.*" Roelof looked at Ernst from one eye. Ernst reassured him, "You just watch me. I'll show you."

◆   ◆   ◆

Clara scanned every street crossing for the hooded man. Rain gathered at her eyebrows and trickled into her eyes. She turned a corner, and the arches of the Katherijnepoort gate came into view. She started running toward the bridge, looking every direction. But the rain had cleared most of the people from the streets.

About a block behind her, two boys, one tall, one short, scampered across the wet street. Clara didn't stand in the middle of the bridge, since the hooded man ran when he saw them. She waited off to the side, along the canal wall. Watching. Watching. Nothing.

Ernst and Roelof didn't know where she had gone, so they walked right up the middle of the street. In a moment she saw them, not realizing who they were at first. Then she gave her signature "beeee-ooooh-wit" call. Ernst turned and ran toward her, shouting and waving, "I'm hungry" as he approached. Roelof joined in. When the boys stood in front of her, Roelof shouted, "I'm a dumbhead." Ernst explained the language shift in Clara's ear. But she wasn't at all interested in playing, though she didn't destroy Ernst's fun. Ernst now realized she had been crying.

"I'm a dumbhead," said Roelof again.

"I'll bet you are," Clara said without interest. She gave Roelof some leftover pastry from her pocket and looked away from the boys. Ernst gave Roelof an I-told-you-so look.

"What are you doing here? What's the matter?" Ernst asked her.

She didn't answer. He pressed her again. "I can't say," she said sharply. "But I'm looking for that hooded man. Have you seen him?"

Ernst shook his head. Rain dripped off him. He

shook his head harder, like a dog, and more water flew off. Clara stepped away.

"He's not Father, you know," Ernst said, digging a bit.

"What-do-you-know?" she snapped. She looked away, and Ernst shrugged his shoulders at Roelof.

Roelof said, "The Princess is rude. Let's go spy." They left her alone there without a word and headed home. She stayed there leaning against the wall for almost the entire afternoon. She rarely looked about anymore for the hooded man.

When the rain started to thin out, she suddenly stood up, soaked to the skin, and started running back to the uncles' studio. Street after street sped by until she came to the studio door. She held her side, trying to make the ache go away. She listened at the door to see if anyone was inside, then slowly opened the door. No one was there. She crossed straight over to the Soomerschoon and lifted the pot above her head ready to smash it on the ground. The tulip bobbed back and forth in the air.

*Patience,* she said to herself. *Patience, patience, patience. I'll show them patience.* She brought the Soomerschoon back down to the counter. She opened and closed several tool drawers, finally finding a little cutting blade. Her clothes were still wet but not dripping. They slowed her movements a bit. She paused in front of the Soomerschoon, and then shot out her hand with the blade in a silver arc. The tulip stood there for just a moment, then separated, bent, and bounced on the counter. *Father was here all the time.* She cut the bulb across the base, and the petals fell apart. *Cruel to all of us.* She took the petals one by one and started slicing them with the blade into thin crimson and cream strips. She scooped up the petal strips in one hand, and with the other, she took a paint brush and spread some sticky oil onto the dark counter top. Then she began setting individual strips down in the shapes of letters, writing a note to her uncles, strip by strip. The note took over an hour to write, and she didn't know what she would have done if the uncles had shown up midway. When she was done, there in slices of Soomerschoon strips was her message: *The letter was old and useless. The man says Father has been hiding in town from us!!! I've gone for the third letter. Please explain to Mother. Please don't follow or he will destroy the third letter.* Then she left.

When the uncles returned soon, it took them a while to run across the petal note on the counter. Caspar called Hendrick over to see it.

"This is rather criminal," said Caspar.

Hendrick came over, and his whole body jerked when he saw it. He put his hand over his forehead and doubled over as if he were winded. He crouched at the knees for several moments and then stood up.

"If it's true, it's very cruel," said Caspar.

"I'm sure the Soomerschoon didn't like it," said Hendrick. "At least it took plenty of patience to write this."

Caspar breathed deeply. "Patience," he said, "and pride."

A short while later, Clara pounded on the front door of the orphanage. Margarieta opened the door and curtseyed.

"I'm so glad to see you again," said Margarieta. She came out and hugged Clara, whose arms became stiff boards again. As she led Clara in, Margarieta started chattering about all sorts of things—weather, flowers, her dress. All sorts of children pressed around them from every side. "I can't wait to be in the painting competition with you," said Margarieta.

"*Against* me, you mean," said Clara.

"Oh, do we have to say that? Whatever, whatever," Margarieta laughed in between words. "All the teachers say that I'm better than you, but I can't believe that. That's so silly. Can you believe it?" Clara didn't answer. "Yes, I've probably had more years of practice, but that's Mr. Liebens pressing, not me. I think you'll do just fine. And if you don't win this one, there will be plenty of others. You have many good years ahead of you, I'm sure." She hugged Clara again. "So many people have told me that I have the soul of a painter." She laughed. "I don't know what that means, but I suppose it helps. Have people said that about you? Do you have the soul of a painter?" More giggling.

"No, but I think I have a cold," said Clara.

Then Clara said she wanted to see Mr. Liebens. "Of course you do. Wait here, dear," said Margarieta and floated down the hall and up the stairs. A moment later, Margarieta stuck only her hand around the corner and beckoned Clara to follow. Margarieta laughed at her beckoning joke and hugged Clara again. Liebens was sitting at his desk when Clara entered.

"What may I do for you, my dear Clara?"

"What do I have to do for the third letter?"

Margarieta asked if she should leave. Yes, leave, was the answer. When Margarieta had gone, Liebens' face changed.

"Time is short. Life is short. The competition is next week. Clara, you've been so busy making my crimson that you haven't had time to practice. But I don't want to take any chances. These orphans, like Margarieta, need to win. That's all they have." He watched her face to make sure she was following him. "I'll give you the third letter, if you decline to take part in the painting competition."

Clara didn't hesitate. "No, I'm sorry I can't do that, Mr. Liebens. It's all I have."

"All you have? You have *everything*. These orphans have nothing." He ran his hand over his head, his face reddening. "Your house is floating in money and paintings and food. And you have the gall to stand there— a bratty little rich girl—and deny these orphans something beautiful. Oh, how well I see how hard it is for the rich to enter the kingdom of heaven."

Clara thought of Judas worrying about the poor. She said, "I don't even know if the last letter is helpful at all." Clara couldn't believe she was saying this. She had to have that letter.

"Oh, I assure you it is very helpful," said Liebens.

"Excuse me, sir, but that's what you led me to believe about the second letter. I can't trust you. You joined my father in lying to us. What kind of a man does that?" She turned to leave, but stopped. "And besides, winning that competition will be the only way a girl like me can get back at you for what you've done." In her head, Clara was arguing against herself, stop, stop, but her legs kept moving.

"Wait," said Liebens, rubbing his hands. "If the competition isn't worth the letter, then perhaps something less." *Yes, yes, yes, offer something less, please,* Clara begged inside her head. "How about giving Margarieta some lessons on color mixing? I'm weak in that area, and you are strong. Show her the basics. Show her how to mix some blues and greens and the Battista crimson, and then I'll hand over the letter to you."

*Don't say no, Don't say no,* was ringing inside Clara. "You want me to help Margarieta beat me in the competition?" asked Clara.

"Sounds a bit odd, doesn't it?" said Liebens. "But yes, for the letter, you know."

Inside Clara's head, the war was still waging. *Stay away from Margarieta. You'll be tempted to slap her at some point. Don't say no. Last chance to find Father. Mother has given up.*

"My time is short," said Liebens in a bored way. "I won't make you another offer."

Clara stared at her shoes, then turned and left without a word. When she reached the outside, the sun's rays were making odd lines. She finally breathed out. To her left there was movement. She turned and saw Ernst and Roelof coming up to her, breaking into this other world from a good world.

Ernst waved at her and patted his head, "I'm hungry."

Roelof waved too and patted his head, "I'm hungry."

Clara replied, "I'm hungry to see you too. But I'm not a dumbhead," she smiled.

"I am," said Roelof.

"We knew you'd be here," said Ernst.

"We're good spies," said Roelof.

Then Ernst's face fell serious. "I miss Father. Have you found him yet?" Ernst had cut through so much of the angry fog in her thinking. They both wanted Father.

"No, I haven't found him," she said. "But I'm close. I need you two to go on a mission. I have to go back inside, but I want you two to go and find that hooded man by the bridge. Find out where he lives." She looked in their eyes. "This isn't a game," she added. "This is very important, and I need your help."

The boys' eyes brightened. A real mission. They left without saying good-bye, running and greeting people with declarations of hunger.

Clara turned and opened the door herself. She quietly walked down the hallway, then up the stairs to Liebens' office. She knocked on the open door and saw him talking to Margarieta and some other girls. They all looked up, waiting for her to speak.

"I'll do it," Clara said to Liebens. Margarieta clapped her hands and bounced. "We start tomorrow, here," said Clara. "Be ready Margarieta." Margarieta started hugging the girls around her. Mr. Liebens smiled at Clara and nodded slowly.

# CHAPTER EIGHT

# Family Secrets

This was just too big. Clara's back ached from thinking and worrying about all this. As she walked toward her home, the questions bounced back and forth. *Who is telling the truth? Who isn't? Is Father in town? Is he alive? I can't argue with Liebens anymore. That's Father's job, if he were here, not a thirteen-year-old's. Even if Liebens burns the letter, I have to speak to Mother.*

Clara stumbled through the door and found Mother and the uncles sitting around the table, a cloud of tobacco smoke hung around the uncles' heads. Clara saw their faces and dropped to the floor sobbing, a puddle of skirts. All three chairs screeched on the floor as the three ran over to her.

"I just can't do it anymore," she said. They took her upstairs to her bed and made her lie down. She spoke to them from her pillow. She explained everything that had happened, even naming Mr. Liebens, and apologized to her mother for not telling her sooner. She had been too afraid that Father would have been lost forever. Mother stroked Clara's hair and told her that the uncles had kept her posted on everything apart from these last few turns.

"Nothing happens in my house that I don't know about," Mother said. "Where do you think that Soomerschoon came from? It didn't just pop onto the counter."

The uncles even looked surprised at this. They stared at Mother and let their pipes droop at odd angles. Clara put her hand over her own eyes and laughed lightly.

"You were so determined," said Mother. "I didn't want to squash your hope for your father. You had to learn that for yourself. Now I think you have, and we need to put an end to this game with Mr. Liebens."

A worried frown cut across Clara's face. She was relieved and misunderstood by Mother at the same time. Mother's knowledge had removed this ox from Clara's back, but she still wanted that third letter and that hooded man. Clara wished she could turn back the discussion a bit.

Mother said, "I'll go and talk to Mr. Liebens tomorrow, and you can go prepare for the competition."

"Please, no, Momma." Clara sat up and grabbed her mother's hand. "Now that you know everything, I am a thousand times better. But I haven't given up hope. Father is alive somewhere."

"It's not good for you to be like this, Clara. It's making you sick."

"Please, Momma, I'm much better. You've given me new life. You've cleared things up in my head. You've been behind me all the way. Please, please, let me finish now."

"This is silly, Clara. What is going to happen to you when you realize that your father is dead? You won't be able to go on. He's *gone*, Clara. You can't go on living like this forever. He was my heart and soul—" and Mother broke off. She covered her face with her hands and wept.

The uncles didn't know what to do, so they just leaned forward. Clara stroked her mother's hair. Only Mother's quiet sobs broke the silence. A few moments passed, then Mother raised her head. "The Lord gives and the Lord takes away," she said. "I'll weep with you when you understand that, Clara, but for now you do what you have to do to get that ridiculous letter." Mother stood and left the room, leaving a light wake of French perfume that Clara breathed in, eyes closed.

Clara arrived at the orphanage early the next day underneath broad sunshine. Her first rule was that Margarieta had to stop hugging her. It was Friday, and the competition was set for the following Friday. So they would have lessons two days this week, and then skipping Sunday, they would have four meetings next week, ending on Thursday. Margarieta and Clara would work on colors every morning, and then Margarieta would practice actual painting with Mr. Liebens in the afternoons.

Before starting the first lesson, Margarieta and Clara talked about the competition. Margarieta went on about the rounds of painting the participants would have to pass through, and then the prizes. First prize was that little known Bartolomeo Manfredi painting. Second prize was a lute from Germany. The third prize winner got to borrow the horse used as the model in the competition for a week. It was a wonderful chestnut horse from a wealthy Utrecht merchant's ranch, but just for a week.

First, Clara taught Margarieta how to mix black. Margarieta sat wide-eyed, as Clara explained that there were several kinds of black—lampblack, ivory black, blue black, red black, and others. The best black pigment came from the teeth of walruses, but those were hard to come by. Normal coal made a sort of brownish-black, which is good for face shadows. Black chalk ground in oil dries easily and spreads well and is good for painting satin clothing. Margarieta kept laughing and asking Clara to make it simpler. They quickly went from talk to practice, with Margarieta taking notes the whole time.

On Saturday they would work on mixing whites, Monday—blues, Tuesday—reds (including Battista crimson), Wednesday—greens, and Thursday—yellows. The most important lesson, Clara kept saying, with a bit of an upturned head, was patience. If you didn't have patience, you couldn't make good colors.

At every lesson, Margarieta's girlfriends sat in the opposite corner of the room, whispering and giggling among themselves. During short breaks, Margarieta joined these giggling sessions for a few minutes while Clara prepared for the next shade. Clara resisted the temptation to go over and ask what was so funny all the time. She knew they had nothing important to whisper about.

At the end of Tuesday's class, one of the girls stood up and said to Clara, "Do you know you have a red stripe on your cheek?" The girl turned back to a barrage of supporting giggles from her friends. Clara just smiled and didn't respond. She felt a little sorry for them.

The next day, Wednesday, the whole group of girls came over during the lesson and stood behind Clara and Margarieta. Clara was explaining how to make certain shades of green.

"You can make one of the best greens from verdigris"—blank look from Margarieta—"you know, that greenish tinge on copper. If you scrape that off and let it sit in vinegar for a long time, it makes little green crystals. Leonardo da Vinci said that as soon as you grind these verdigris crystals, you must mix them with a varnish, or else they'll fade horribly. He's right." The girls behind them whispered. "But it all takes patience. I may not be able to paint the best, but I've got patience, and that's what counts with colors." The girls behind them giggled and whispered.

"Ladies," said Clara, "would you mind not standing by us? We're almost done, then you can all go giggle until you're verdigris."

"Who do you think you are?" said one of the girls.

"You think you are so special—Miss Patience," said another rolling her eyes.

"Too bad you won't be in the competition," said another; the others laughed. Margarieta laughed along with them. "It would be nice to see your patient nose lose," said another.

"Oh, I'll be there," said Clara, cleaning up. The girls went silent.

Margarieta spoke next, a little troubled. "But Mr. Liebens told us you were not taking part."

"No, I'll be there, God willing." The other girls giggled some more and rolled their eyes again, silently mimicking the way Clara spoke. Just then Mr. Liebens entered the room to check up on things and ask a question. He carried a canvas marked with paint samples.

"Are we done?"

Clara said they were. The group of girls listened in.

"Tell me, Clara, I can't put my finger on it, but I've been testing these paints you've taught Margarieta to mix. And something seems off. They don't look like the paints I used to get from your father."

Clara swallowed and held the canvas up to the light. "They seem all right to me," she said.

"No, look here. This is an old green from your

father, and this is one just mixed. It seems, I don't know, shinier or something. Not deep."

One of the girls from the pack spoke up. "Mr. Liebens, sir, she doesn't know everything."

Another spoke in mock defense of Clara. "She is just a beginner."

But Clara remembered the problem. It was the same secret that the uncles had told her to put in the crimson—spike oil. But that was a family secret.

"I *do* know the problem, but I'm not allowed to say. I can fix it secretly," she said.

"Now, now, girl," said Liebens, huffing a bit, "that wasn't our deal. You agreed to teach Margarieta proper colors. This isn't proper. You're breaking your part of the deal. Are you purposely trying to make Margarieta lose the competition? That would be low," stretching the last word. The girls tsked-tsked melodramatically.

Clara thought to herself, *how I would like to quiet them; no spike, no letter; if Father is in town tricking us, then he deserves to have his secrets revealed; if he's dead, then he wouldn't care.*

Liebens came closer and whispered, "Look, unless you tell me how to fix this, you won't get your letter."

Clara was tired of all of this. More from wanting to show these girls she knew what she was talking about, she walked over to her supply box and pulled out the bottle of golden spike oil. She slapped it into Liebens' hand.

"Put four drops in every cup. It will remove the shininess." With that she picked up her things and left for the day.

On Thursday, the last day for Margarieta's lessons, Clara's tone was very cool. She still bore the heaviness of revealing her father's secret. But she made up all sorts of justifications in her mind. They fell apart rather quickly though. She knew if she had listened to her mother, she wouldn't even have been here. So she moved through Margarieta's lesson on yellows more quickly than others. She didn't smile once; Margarieta kept her distance too. Near the end of the lesson, though, a round boy brought a message in to Clara. She read it and crumpled it. "Where is he?" she asked the boy. He pointed to the front door. Margarieta's face was all question marks. Clara ran from the room.

Clara could hardly breathe as she ran to the door, pushing past the children lining the corridors. She burst out of the front door onto the street, looking this way and that. Across the street, the hooded man stood with his back to her, talking to Ernst and Roelof.

Ernst came running over to her and said, "You won't believe what I found."

Clara straightened her skirts and walked stiffly over to him. But even before she got there, she knew it couldn't be her father. She would have been shocked if it was. A step behind him, he turned and pulled back his hood. He smiled at her, and he did look like Father, even from the front. But of course it wasn't. She had changed her expectations so quickly in the walk from the door that she wasn't disappointed. She realized she would have been terribly angry if it had been her father, tricking them like this. Instead of killing hope, this man resurrected it. He spoke to her.

"Lutes of the moon, yeh, yeh, yeh, refuse to pick up their trash, yeh," he said. Clara smiled a smile of confusion.

"Excuse me?" she said.

The man spoke with wide eyes. "I once ate a cow in

a stream, yeh. My mother was a book, my father a grass pony."

Ernst came up beside them. "He's a funny old guy, isn't he?"

"Soldiers hide in our yellow funny," said the man.

She pulled Ernst aside, whispering. "It's not funny. He's mad. Take him back home, now." Clara said she had to go back to her lesson. Ernst and Roelof followed the man, skipping down the road, all three of them greeting people with "I'm hungry" waves and pats on their heads.

Back inside the orphanage, Clara sat down again with Margarieta, who had kept working on mixing. She was quieter than before. "I think you should speak to Mr. Liebens," Margarieta said. "About tomorrow. The girls asked him." Clara got up without a word and made her way through the halls to his office. As she climbed the stairs, she tried to figure out the best way to start this talk. She appeared in his doorway. He invited her in. She spied the chocolate coat still on his chair.

"Mr. Liebens, sir, I've almost finished the last lesson with Margarieta. May I have my letter now?"

"But you haven't finished your end of the bargain yet," he said with a chuckle. She sensed another one of those conversations, and her stomach turned. *Mother was right,* she thought.

"I don't understand," she said.

"Your agreement was to teach and decline the competition. But—"

Clara cut him off. "You know that's not true!" she said.

"Please, my dear, I have a much better practiced memory than you do, and I distinctly remember our agreement. I wish you had written it down because now you'll think that I'm twisting things, when I'm not. I'm sticking to our agreement." He sighed. "Why don't we ever write these things down? Now I get blamed for your irresponsibility."

"Please give me my letter," she said, tightlipped.

"No, get out of my office. You twist and lie and always get your proud little way. Not this time, girlie. Get out." He closed the door behind her.

Clara walked slowly down the hall and turned the corner. She wanted to beat her head against a wall. She realized things would happen seconds before they did. But that wasn't enough time. Then she heard Liebens open his door and come tromping down the hallway. She hid behind an open door. *Think, think, think,* she said. *He's going to give painting lessons. The letter is in his office. The hooded man wasn't Father. Liebens only speaks lies. What is my only comfort in life and death? My things are back with Margarieta. Got to get them, or he'll come back. I've got to get the letter from Pharaoh.*

A moment later, Clara walked into the room where Liebens was starting the painting lesson with Margarieta. "Yes, would you please carry your things away?" he said. He shoved her box with his foot. Margarieta wouldn't look her in the eye. Clara quickly picked up her things and left. Liebens called after her, as a sort of test, "Will we see you tomorrow at the competition?"

"I don't know, sir," she said. He growled and went back to painting. Clara still hadn't tried to get the letter. But now she was walking toward the door, and once through it, she would probably never be let back in again. This was her last chance. She stepped into a side room and set her supply box and bags in a corner. Then she walked back up the corridor, not knowing what she would do. Sometimes children passed her, but they were used to seeing her, as were other teachers. She came to the edge of the door where Liebens and Margarieta were. She had to get across in order to get to his office, but he was facing the door opening. She could listen for him to turn his head, but Margarieta might see her. She could wait for a small crowd of children to stoop behind, but that might take too long, and they might give her away.

She was waiting for Liebens to drop a paint brush or some other distraction, when in the middle of the thought he did just that. She didn't have time to think; her legs hopped her across the doorway, and she stood cringing, waiting for a shout or a shuffle. But nothing came. She needed to breathe but kept walking quietly down the hall instead. She climbed the stairs, almost crawling, and turned down his hall. His door kept coming closer. Her ear was constantly behind her, listening, discerning. She walked past Liebens' office around a hall corner. She had seen that his door was closed. She listened and then walked by again and tried the door. It was unlocked. Before she could think, she was inside, breathing giant buckets of air. She quietly closed the door. For a moment, she stared at the paintings on the four walls, all packed tightly together, floor to ceiling, except for two windows on the far side. She snapped her head to the chocolate-colored jacket still hanging on the chair. Moving quickly to it, she reached inside and pulled out the letter. It was like gold in her hands. It had body and weight and hope. She held it to her lips.

But time was short. She had to get out. She had just pressed the letter into her skirt pocket, when she heard something odd. A key turning in the office door. She ducked behind the desk. But the door didn't open. *Think, think, think.* She remembered that no key had been on the outside of the door when she had come in. Someone had just put one in and turned it. She walked like a hunting cat to the door and listened. She bent over and looked through the keyhole. It was blocked by a key for a moment, then it was removed. Her blood beat in her ears. She could see bits of Liebens' clothes through the keyhole. He was just standing there, breathing. Clara touched the top of the doorknob lightly. He must have seen it move ever so slightly.

"I hope you enjoy your letter," he said through the door. Clara jiggled the doorknob forcefully now.

"You can't leave me in here," she said back.

"I can leave you in there until the competition is over. It will help you keep your promise to me," he said.

"But when it's over, I'll tell everyone what you did." Clara wished she could have taken those words back.

"Go ahead. I'll tell them that some orphan boy was playing a prank, and that I'm awfully sorry for you. But why was she in my office alone anyway?" Silence. Clara couldn't think of anything else to say. "Well, enough said. Have a good night. I'll come for you after the competition." He started walking away, then his steps doubled-back. "Oh, and enjoy the riddle."

"What riddle?" she asked.

"The one on the letter you took from my pocket." He paused. "You don't think I'd leave your father's letter there, do you?"

Clara pulled the letter out of her pocket. Liebens walked away whistling a cheery tune. She opened it and saw it wasn't her father's handwriting. It was Liebens'. She crumpled it into a ball. *After all this*, she thought, and she didn't even have her father's letter.

# CHAPTER NINE

# Painted Prison

*Oh, how I hate riddles,* thought Clara. She had already checked the window and any other way to escape. Then, for the longest time, she sat on the floor with her back against Liebens' door. As the afternoon wore on, and the sun faded, darkness took up posts in the corners of the room. The riddle from Liebens still lay crumpled on the floor a few steps in front of her. For a while she dozed. When she woke, her rest had made her think of escaping again. She began by searching for a second key. She checked Liebens' desk drawers and the pockets in his jacket. Nothing. She checked odd spaces to hide keys, like above the door and under decorative boxes from China. Nothing. It was getting darker, so she started a fire in the fireplace and lit as many oil lamps and candles as she could. When she was done, it looked like a royal funeral, all lit up in flames of gold and white, dancing shadows across the paintings. It made them take on a different life.

The last bit of sunlight slipped through the windows, and she went over to look through them again. From the second story where she was, she looked down on the orphanage garden. She pushed the windows open and checked again whether she could jump. From the very first, she had ruled out screaming for help. That might get her out of the room, but it would almost certainly mean she would never see her father's letter. She had to wait for Liebens or escape quietly. She left the windows ajar so the evening air would come in. She thought of Father's letter—she had seen it once when Liebens had shown her the second letter. She now remembered it had looked different than the riddle letter she had taken from Liebens' jacket. *Where was that letter?* She hated riddles so much that she hadn't even wanted to read it. She couldn't solve them most of the time, though Ernst was a whiz at them. Riddles always seemed to include some twisted bit of information that only the writer knew. So why even try? But what else could she do?

She left the window and picked up the crumpled wad of thick, cracked paper. Unfolding it next to an oil lamp, she studied it. Liebens had written:

*Clara, I knew you would try to take what you hadn't earned. So I hid your father's letter at the end of a trail of riddles. Along the way you should find the key out of this room too, but you'll be too late for the competition. Be sure to hand over all the riddles to the man waiting at the end, or else you won't get your precious letter. Here is riddle number one: Heidelberg ten, lack nine, picks this painting in reverse, if you're an ancient man.*

She crumpled the riddle again and tossed it over her shoulder. "Painting-shmainting. Just great! Now I remember why I hate riddles!" she said aloud. *Liebens just wants me to waste time figuring it out,* she thought.

She started searching for a key again. This time, though, she started opening all his books. She opened each one upside down and turned the pages with her thumb. Perhaps a key would drop to the ground. It took her an hour to get through every book. But nothing. No key. And the sun had completely vanished. She shut the windows to keep the coolness out. *Why aren't Mother and the uncles out looking for me?*

She sat by the fireplace and read the riddle again in its light. *Heidelberg ten, lack nine, picks this painting in reverse, if you're an ancient man.* She memorized it without thinking. *An ancient man. A painting.* She picked up an oil lamp and walked from wall to wall studying the paintings, looking for Adam and old men. Liebens had still lifes, landscapes, biblical scenes, and portraits. She paced the walls several times, but nothing jumped out at her. A few paintings had ancient men, but they had no key or note attached. For a very high painting that pictured Samson, she pulled a desk over and stacked a chair on it. But it had nothing. *Heidelberg ten, lack nine.* She looked around Liebens' books for a text on the history of Heidelberg, Germany, and then she looked for a copy of the Heidelberg Catechism. She didn't find either one.

*Heidelberg ten, lack nine, picks this painting in reverse, if you're an ancient man.* She said it over and over, wishing Ernst was there. She tried different things in her head and finally stumbled upon, *ten lack nine is like ten minus nine, or one. Heidelberg one. The first question of the Heidelberg Catechism.* But as soon as she had this thought, she became angry again. "Just like Liebens," she said. "My father in the balance, and he wants to punish me with a lesson." She shook the paper and thought in mocking, sing-song thoughts, *I can see it now preached from all the pulpits. Clara of Utrecht saved her father because she knew her catechism. Children everywhere should learn their catechism so they too can escape villains' riddles plaguing the land!*

When her disgust cooled, her thoughts went back to Liebens' riddle. She recited the first question of the Heidelberg Catechism: "What is your only comfort in life and death? Answer: That I am not my own. . . ."

She said it all the way through while thinking of the last part of the riddle: *picks this painting in reverse, if you're an ancient man.* In her mind she tried to reverse each line of Heidelberg One and find a connection to an ancient man: "soul and body, death and life, free and blood, head and fall, ready and eternal." She tried saying some lines altogether backwards: "soul and body with belong but" and "devil the of power the all from" and *not a hair can fall from my head* became, "head can fall from hair." That last wasn't exactly in reverse, but it made her think of several paintings.

She said it over and over: "head can fall from hair." Then it struck her, *an ancient man is a skull without hair.* She ran along the wall, trying to remember a particular painting. She saw it up high and pulled the small desk over, stacking a chair on it like before. They wobbled as she climbed higher and higher. Then face to face with it, she stared at a painting of a young woman, with a blue wrap and head covering, sitting at a desk, her head in sadness. The background was dark, and a candle cast stark light and shadows onto the woman's face. In her hand, the woman held a skull— "head can fall from hair," said the riddle's catechism.

Clara ran her finger along the shadows— "Caravaggisti" she spoke through a smile. *Perfect houding.* She glanced at the artist's initials. She knew of him from church—H. Ter Brugghen. She was so taken with the glorious shadow work on the woman's face that she almost forgot her mission. She steadied herself on the chair and looked at the frame for a key or a note. Nothing. She ran her hand around it as far as she could and then tipped up the bottom of the frame. A folded piece of paper dropped out and skidded down across the faces of the paintings below. It landed on the corner of the oriental rug and seemed to call to her.

◆ ◆ ◆

For the past seven hours Mother, the uncles, Ernst, and Roelof had been searching for Clara up and down the streets of Utrecht. No one had seen her. They had gone to the orphanage first, but Liebens had told them that she had left earlier in the day. Ernst went to all the places they often visited, but nothing. They had checked barges, St. Luke's, the Buurkerk, friends' houses, nothing.

At last they spoke to magistrate officers who said they would keep their eyes open but that the family had to go inside now because it was dark. When he got home, Ernst asked if Roelof could spend the night. They had a spy mission in the morning. Uncle Hendrick gladly agreed.

Clara climbed down from the chair ever so carefully and picked up the note. She opened it, expecting to have it tell her the location of the key. But instead it read, *That was an easy one. Riddle Two is: Its apostles less one, then by the miracle loaves, was shown by the prime of Utrecht.*

Clara sat against the wall and put her head to her knees. "If only the magistrate would ban riddles," she said. "Then we could imprison riddle-crafters, or at least thunk their heads." But she had beaten one already, and now she was more familiar with Liebens' ways. She stared at it for a while, and it started making more sense. He was probably still thinking of the Heidelberg Catechism with the number part: *Its apostles less one, then by the miracle loaves. Well, the first part was easily eleven. Twelve Apostles minus one. But what were the miracle loaves? Loaves in the tabernacle in the Old Testament? Moses' manna in the desert? Christ's loaves and fishes?*

She went over to Liebens' desk and opened his large
Bible. She started searching in Exodus for the number
of the loaves of shewbread that sat in the tabernacle.
She couldn't find an exact number. So she turned to
the New Testament and looked for the number of
loaves Christ used to feed the thousands.

Clara started skimming through Matthew for the
miracle account. It took a while, but when she came to
chapter fourteen, there it was: five loaves fed five thousand people: *Its apostles less one, then by the miracle
loaves. Eleven by five, which is fifty-five.* Now she had to
remember question fifty-five of the Heidelberg. She
didn't memorize by numbers but by questions. *Was it
"What do you believe concerning the Holy Spirit?" or
"What comfort does the resurrection of the body offer you?"
No. Nothing in those questions seemed to connect with
the part of the riddle that talks about "the prime of Utrecht." What was that? a time in history? a building? the
Chief magistrate? a former bishop?* Then it clicked.

She stood up and started looking for the painting
she had seen five or six times now. It was low, she remembered, on the other side of the room. *There.* Back
in the corner under the window hung a copy of
Droochsloot's *Saint Martin Dividing His Cloak.* St.
Martin was the first man, the prime man, of Utrecht—
its patron saint. He was a nobleman who had ridden
into the city of Amiens and found worthy beggars seeking his help. He clothed them with his crimson cloak
and gave them food and wine. Heidelberg fifty-five, it
was, that said "everyone is duty-bound to use his gifts
readily and cheerily for the benefit and well-being of
the other members." *Its apostles less one, then by the
miracle loaves, was shown by the prime of Utrecht.*

She reached down and unhooked the painting from

the wall. There on the back a note was stuck. This was getting easy. She glanced out the window, and all Utrecht was asleep; the stars were high.

She peeled off the note and unfolded it, knowing it had to be another riddle, hoping for the location of the key. This one read: *If you're here, then try riddle three: leaf and blade, rain and drought, sit veiled in its box, your key sits beneath Van der Ast's true spring.*

"The key," she spoke aloud. "Van der Ast. We visited his house. But the painting he showed us wasn't his own. It was Bosschaert's. I need to find a Van der Ast painting. He painted flowers too. And that involves spring." Liebens' had several flower paintings, only one by Van der Ast. *Liebens didn't think I'd know this one. Too easy.*

The Van der Ast painting was on a different wall, midway up. She just needed to stand on a chair. Before she lifted it she closely looked at the painting. It was a vase full of flowers from every season, smoky background. The vase in the painting sat on a shelf that held shells and a grasshopper. Hanging out of the vase toward the left was a Soomerschoon, with perfect crimson stripes. Clara wanted to hold it, breathe that tulip again. She didn't know the other flowers. She knew their names, of course, carnation, rose, iris. But she had lived the Soomerschoon. It had given itself to her so grandly, offering its color. She knew every part of it, every curve and bend, thinness, thickness, inside, outside, dark, light, faint aroma, and then she had killed it in anger. Cut it into strips. She allowed herself to touch the image of the tulip in the painting.

"The key!" she said. "I need the key." She unhooked the painting from the wall and peered around the frame. No note. But no key either. She carried it down, coming down carefully off the chair. She turned it this way and that and even loosened the frame. Nothing. She searched the surrounding paintings and went back to the riddle: *leaf and blade, rain and drought, sit veiled in its box, your key sits beneath Van der Ast's true spring.* "Here it is. But no key."

She paced in a circle, reciting different parts of the riddle. It all kept pointing back to this same painting. *Perhaps Liebens had just stopped; no key at all.* It was now long past midnight, and she was still locked in. She started removing every painting from the wall, checking every frame for the key. In another hour, all the paintings were on the floor pointing different directions, as if a wagon had spilled a load of them. Clara sat weeping in the middle. On her lap sat Van der Ast's flower painting.

She wept because she was trapped. Wept to be with her mother and father. Wept against the riddle. The opening lines of the riddle floated through her hazy mind again: *leaf and blade, rain and drought.* Like Liebens' other riddles, these also came from the Heidelberg. She had recited the whole answer for question twenty-seven several times as she searched the paintings.

She stared at the painting and recited, "as with His hand, He still upholds heaven and earth and all creatures, and so governs them that,

> leaf and blade,
> rain and drought,
> fruitful and barren years,
> food and drink,
> health and sickness,
> riches and poverty,
> indeed, all things,

come not by chance but by
His fatherly hand."

As she stared at the image of the Soomerschoon, she realized it had lost its first magic. The more she looked at it, the more she saw that it didn't capture the real Soomerschoon she had held. The painting even seemed a little cold and lifeless now. *As with His hand,' says the catechism, 'leaf and blade.'*

"There's only one real artist," she said to herself slowly. *Who was I to boast of my crimson, my patience? It all looks so small now next to any part of creation. He's the artist; we're the idiot copiers. Who am I to "darken counsel" by pale colors? 'When I consider the work of Your fingers, the moon and the stars. . . . What is man that You are mindful of him?'And I killed His artwork without a thought.*

"Patient and proud," she whispered aloud. "I deserve to miss the competition and lose a father. No respect. I hate painting. I'm done with it." She lay back amid her skirts and the paintings and closed her eyes. Before she fell fully asleep, she said to no one through a long sigh, "I knew I hated riddles."

On the other side of Utrecht, Roelof was snoring next to Ernst. Ernst couldn't sleep, even apart from the snoring. At least he thought he hadn't slept a wink, but he had, off and on. The hooded man kept popping into his dreams. "A bridge of daisied milk supports a dog's lip," and other such sayings kept sneaking into his head. Ernst would sit up looking for the old man, and then try to lay back down.

Nearer to dawn, Ernst was wide awake, wondering where his sister was. He knew he had to try the orphanage again. He needed a little more light. He watched the darkness give way to light gold in the sky, and he tried to shake Roelof awake.

Roelof shook his hand in the air and mumbled, "my hair is wet." That was just sleep talk. Ernst thought about what he was going to do and realized it would be better to leave Roelof behind. Sliding like a spy out of bed and then out of the room, Ernst tried not to make the stairs creak as he went down. But when he was halfway down, his bedroom door opened, and Roelof came out crying and searching. Ernst waved him quiet. He started to tell Roelof he couldn't go on the spy mission, but he knew his cousin would throw a fit. No time for lessons on manhood now. Amid a flurry of whispers on the stairs, Ernst gave in. Roelof's frown gave way to a smile, and the boys went downstairs and inhaled some pastries from the kitchen. They made their way across town to the orphanage through the cool morning air.

Brightness was entering Liebens' office, but Clara was sound asleep. She was dreaming that she was calling to Ernst across a canal with her "beeee-ooooh-wit" call. In her dream she did it again and again, but he didn't hear her. Finally, she heard the sound, but it didn't seem to come from her dream. It happened a couple more times, and the dream's mistake made her open her eyes. Nothing.

Then she heard it. "Beeee-ooooh-wit" from outside. It was getting fainter. She pushed some paintings out of the way and scrambled to her feet, tiptoeing through others all the way to the window. She stared out to make sure it was clear, then she opened the window and gave a low "beeee-ooooh-wit" call in reply. She hoped it sounded like some morning bird, but it did nothing of the kind. She heard some running, and then another "beeee-ooooh-wit" from down the street. She answered, and another one came closer. Clara stuck her head out of the window. She called out again in a higher pitch this time, and someone across the way opened a window and shouted, "Hey, shut up, whoever's doing that!"

Clara cringed, and then she saw Ernst and Roelof beyond a fence. They had both heard the rebuke and covered their mouths. But they furiously waved at Clara. Ernst waved for her to come out the front. She made enough hand signals to say she couldn't. Ernst climbed two fences and pushed and pulled Roelof over the same. Ernst wished more than ever that Roelof hadn't started throwing that fit on the stairs.

After great effort, the boys stood underneath Clara's windows in the orphanage garden. They still weren't close enough to talk though. So Ernst made Roelof wait, and he tried to climb up the brick and stones to the window, at least to get close enough to talk. He pressed his fingers into the narrow spaces between the bricks to get some sort of grip. His body kept pulling him away from the wall.

He pressed his face close to the wall and thought of himself as a lizard. He would move up several bricks and then his fingers would slip, scraping along the bricks. But finally he got high enough—with a more comfortable grip on the first-floor window ledge—that they could whisper.

Clara tried to explain the whole problem to him as quickly as she could. He cut her off midway though, since his fingers ached as they grew whiter. He wanted to hear the last riddle again. She repeated it several times, and then Ernst had to climb down. All the blood had left his arms. He stood in the garden shaking his arms down, then climbed up again.

"It's not a painting," he whispered. She was confused, of course it had to be a painting. He shook his head. "The riddle says the key 'sits beneath Van der Ast's true spring.' A painting isn't a true spring. Find a real flower in the office." He had to climb down again.

Clara looked around frantically, but she knew the room well. There were no real flowers in it. She came back to the window. Ernst expected a "no" answer from her, so before she could speak he said, "look for a box." Clara remembered that's what the riddle said, but she thought that meant a picture frame. She repeated that part of the riddle over and over—*sits veiled in its box, sits veiled in its box.* But she had already looked in every drawer and wardrobe. She started over, this time looking for something like a veil.

She opened and closed all sorts of cabinet doors. But after closing one small side table, she opened it again. Something caught her eye. She swung the door back and forth several times. As she did so, the back moved. She reached in and touched it. The back was made of fabric, the color of the wood.

She stood back a moment and breathed before pulling it away. When she did, there sat a potted flower, a full grown Soomerschoon. She yelped and started to pull it out. As she dragged the small pot, its base bumped and scraped on something hard. It was the key—*leaf and blade, rain and drought, sit veiled in its box, your key sits beneath Van der Ast's true spring.* She was trembling all over. She set the Soomerschoon on the desk. It was too healthy to have been in there more than a day. For a moment she just stared at the tulip. She put her lips to one of its petals. *What is man?* she thought to herself. *Now this is real art. Everything else pales.*

Then she ran the key over to the window and waved it at Ernst. He clapped quietly and motioned her to get out quickly. But as she brought her hand back in the window, she bumped it, and the key twirled down to the boys. She gasped, and Ernst immediately tried to throw it back up. He banged it off the side of the building several times and then took some steps back and threw it past Clara's head into the room.

Clara realized that she had the key but not her father's letter. She turned the Soomerschoon pot around and found a note attached. It was from Liebens, not Father. It read, *I don't suspect you'll ever read this note before I get back. But if you do somehow, the key leads to the letter. To get the letter, you must take this tulip to the van Mander barge waiting at the end of the Nieuwegracht canal. Bring all my notes, and a man there named Otto will trade you for your father's letter.*

Clara gripped the potted Soomerschoon and found the riddles, then set them down again. She found a piece of blank paper in the desk, along with a thin ink brush. She copied the last note word for word onto the sheet. She tried to make it look like Liebens' handwriting, even his signature. Then she picked up the flower and notes and tiptoed through the paintings to the door. The key worked. She breathed. She had been uncertain whether it would work.

She listened down the corridor and the stairs. It sounded like a few children were awake, but they were in the far kitchen. Margarieta and Liebens were probably already setting up at the competition. The first round started early. Clara slithered away through the halls and ran out the front.

# CHAPTER TEN

# Proof Sketches

Ernst and Roelof waited across the street from the orphanage for Clara. Roelof was rubbing his leg. He had caught it while being pulled over one of the fences in the back. A moment later, Clara ran out with her arms full. At the last moment before opening the door she had remembered to pick up her painting box and bags.

She spotted the boys, and none of them talked. She handed off her painting things, but she held on to the Soomerschoon. Then they ran. After a few blocks, Ernst asked where they were going, since he could tell they weren't headed to their home. Clara explained the note between breaths. After a few more blocks, Roelof had to slow down and finally stopped. The other two shifted their things around, and Ernst did his best to carry Roelof. At times Roelof's legs dragged on the ground. It wasn't a pleasant journey. On the way, they passed the edge of the Cathedral plaza where the competition was setting up. Clara could see plenty of people gathering but no sign of Liebens.

A little while later, they arrived at the spot on the Nieuwegracht canal. The sun had fully risen, and they could see the barge they were looking for. It was another flower barge. The boys waited on the bridge while Clara clambered down to the dock. When she got down to the barge, she knocked on a box of sunset orange tulips and called out for anyone on board. A sunburned, bleary-eyed man appeared, and she asked if he was Otto. He didn't answer, just pointed down some steps. She followed his pointing, with the Soomerschoon bouncing back and forth in the pot.

The time to part with the tulip was near, and she tried not to think too much about it. Clara sensed the Soomerschoon looking down its nose at her. She glanced at the tulip petals filtering sunlight, and her eyes traced the crimson curves reaching up to the sky. Even after destroying one Soomerschoon, she knew the privilege of being so close to this one. It would be hard to remove her grip from it, but she kept telling herself that her father's letter was close.

Another sailor pointed her toward Otto, whom she found sitting with his feet up on a barrel, smoking a pipe. Tulips were everywhere, on deck and below deck. This man was wide awake and looked as though he had been waiting. He blew smoke out the side of his mouth and asked her in a raspy voice, "Do you have something for me?"

"Are you Otto?" she asked.

He waved her over closer. "Give me the notes and the Soomer," he said. She took a step back. He laughed a little. "Don't worry. Here's your letter." And he reached behind him and pulled a letter from a slit in the wall.

"Open it and read it to me first," she said. "I'm not handing these over until I'm sure it's the real letter."

Otto looked puzzled. He shrugged and unfolded the letter. He couldn't read smoothly and started reading the first line in a high love-letter voice, "Dear Antonia . . . "

"That's my mother," said Clara.

"Dear Antonia," he started again, "I am writing this

letter through a scribe. I have awakened in Arnhem, a half-day's ride outside Utrecht. The friars are taking good care of me, but it's best I not try to move right now."

"What is the date of that letter?" Clara asked. Otto slowly shrugged and tossed her the paper. He was tired of being a secretary. Clara set down the things she was holding and picked up her father's letter, still watching Otto out of the corner of her eye. The date on the letter was almost two months ago, just before her time in Amsterdam. She turned it over and read her father's script: *My ailment has taken a turn for the worse. The friars tell me I have been in and out of wakefulness for weeks, but mostly sleeping. They don't know what else to do. I can't remember our family address. The friars have contact with Romeyn Liebens at the orphanage there, and they will try to get this note and my old unsent letters to you through him. I don't know how much longer I have. I wish I had never left home. I love you very much. Please tell Clara and Ernst I miss them too much, and I have been praying that they will lead joyful and faithful lives.* Clara frowned at her tears and turned to leave. She stopped and set the Soomerschoon on Otto's barrel and handed him Liebens' notes. He nodded, not even examining them, and she ran up on deck and off the barge.

When she reached Ernst and Roelof waiting at the arc of the bridge, she couldn't talk; she was trying to hold in her sobs. Ernst didn't ask any questions. She handed him the letter, but as he was taking it, all sorts of yelling erupted from the barge. The three children turned and looked over the bridge edge. They saw men running off the barge. Clara grabbed the boys' hands and said "Let's go." Just as she finished her command,

and the three of them turned, the barge gave a low, thunderous rumble. Then it gave three loud explosions. Parts of the deck shot off into the air in a million pieces, as if a volcano had let loose below its deck. The children flinched and ducked behind the bridge wall. Pieces of wood and tulips flew through the air. Clara pushed her body over the boys. With their eyes closed, they could hear bits of things pattering and clattering all around them. When everything stopped falling, they slowly lifted their heads, checking the air through squints. What remained of the barge was sinking into the canal. Clumps of tulips bobbed like ducks on the water.

Ernst looked at Clara, impressed. "How did you do that?" he asked her. She didn't answer.

"Yes, Princess," offered Roelof, big-eyed, willing to bow to her.

"Look," Clara said, "I don't know what happened. The flower I had was just a normal flower."

Clara pulled the boys up, and they all ran off. As they left the area, the children found themselves pressing against crowds of curious people moving toward the explosion.

When they got to the cathedral square, Clara set Roelof down and held her side, resting for a moment. Ernst set her painting things down and plopped down next to Roelof. Ernst was talking at Clara, but her mind was searching for Mother or the uncles in the square. She could see pretty clearly, but they weren't there. And no one in the square seemed to be agitated about the barge explosion. The news hadn't reached there yet.

She started to get up, when Ernst pulled on her. "Answer me," he said. Her eyes asked him for the question again.

"What happened back at the barge?" he repeated. She rubbed her forehead and shook her head in silence.

"We can't stay here," said Clara, still massaging the pain in her side. "I know where Father is. We've got to find Mother and the uncles."

"Where is he?" asked Ernst.

"With some friars in Arnhem."

She stood, and the boys slowly followed. Ernst glanced over to the competition. It still hadn't started. "You know you'll miss the competition," he said to her half-heartedly, just as a test.

"I don't care. The uncles have to take us to Arnhem," she said, but she carefully steered her eyes away from the competition now. She pressed ahead down the street, even though the boys dragged behind. She couldn't slow down, she said. Meet her at home. She ran on, but when she got home, Mother was nowhere to be found. She ran down to the uncles' studio, but it was empty too. Even the neighbors appeared to be gone out to market or maybe to the competition. She ran up and down the quiet street several times, staring up and down other streets in the hope of spotting someone.

Then it struck her that they were probably out frantically searching for her and the boys. But then, they could be anywhere. It might take the whole day to find them. They might be going from church to church or be out at a farm. They might be in a far corner of town. But she knew where father was now, and he couldn't wait, if he was alive at all after two months. She ran back to the uncles' studio and wrote two notes, one she nailed to the uncles' front door, the other to her own door. She couldn't just wait for them to show up, and she couldn't start chasing them blindly all over Utrecht.

As she finished attaching the note to the door, Ernst and Roelof finally arrived, dragging their steps as if they had just crossed a desert.

"I can't find anyone!" she said to them before they spoke. "I'm going back to the competition." The boys looked at each other and groaned. "You two stay here if you want, but I've got to get that Manfredi. It will get me to Father. If the uncles show up, bring them over, and I'll drop everything and go with them. But I don't know of any faster way to get to Father unless Mother and the uncles show up." She picked up her painting supplies and ran off down the street.

When Clara arrived at the platform for her age group, about twenty students were already standing behind easels arranged in a long crescent curve. They were studying the large chestnut-colored horse shifting its feet in front of the platform. Beyond the horse towered the Utrecht cathedral; some were pointing at parts of that. Both the horse and the cathedral would be models for the competition.

Clara spoke to the three judges in charge, moving her hands quickly. Parents and teachers started to clear away from the platform, and Liebens was there. He lingered behind Margarieta and her easel. The two of them were all smiles until Clara's discussion with the judges caught their eyes.

When he saw Clara, Liebens wanted to scream and pull her hair. Through his mind shot images of riddles and St. Martin and the Soomerschoon in that little cabinet. Liebens immediately came down, pushing children out of his way, and joined the conversation with Clara and the judges. Liebens smiled as he reasoned with them. But in the end, the judges made room for another easel and canvas, and they helped Clara up onto the platform. Liebens stood to the side with his arms across his chest.

The main judge—a thin, painfully blond man—explained the plan of the competition. First this group of students would sketch the Utrecht cathedral with as much detail as they could within an hour. The best ten sketches would be allowed to pass on to the second round, but the losing sketch artists would have to leave the platform. For the second round, the remaining ten would sketch the chestnut horse on their largest canvases, and the judges would choose the three best sketches from the ten. Then, finally, using those sketches, the remaining three students would paint the horse in full color, embellishing an interesting background of their own creative choice. Of those three paintings, the best student would receive the Manfredi painting. A German lute went to the second place winner, and the third place student won a week of borrowing the chestnut horse.

When everyone was finally ready, the blond judge shouted "Go!" and the students started sketching the cathedral. Liebens and the giggling girls stood near the front of the platform. He seemed to be staring at Margarieta, but he was actually praying for that Manfredi painting. He could clearly imagine which wall it would hang on. He would even make a wide band of empty wall around it to make it stand out from the other paintings. Then he would catch himself and say that nothing was certain. It was bad luck to have such confidence, so he would go back to praying.

About a half-hour into the sketching time, Ernst and Roelof showed up at the back of the crowd. They came alone. Mother and the uncles were not with them.

During the sketching, no one was allowed to stand behind the platform because that could make the students even more nervous. But as soon as the judges called the end of the first hour, the crowd quickly filled in behind the platform to look up at the cathedral sketches. Liebens stood back in the crowd and tried to compare all of them, especially Margarieta's and Clara's. It was hard to judge from such a distance, except for two or three sketches that were very poor.

Clara's sketch was the last in line, so when the judges finished looking at hers, they left the platform and put their heads together in a meeting. One of them was marking a sheet of paper as the others spoke. They called for quiet, and the chief judge walked to the very beginning of the line and explained that he would point to those students who got to advance to the next round. He started his walk of judgment in front of the platform and passed by the first three students and pointed at the fourth. One of the passed-over boys started to cry, and his father came up and smacked him on the backside of his head for the tears. The judge kept passing some and pointing at a few. Most of the passed-over students showed no expressions. One punched her sketch; another started making excuses about the sun. Margarieta was chosen as a winner, and she teared up a bit. Her friends cheered for her.

Since Clara was last in line, she was trying to count and remember how many had been chosen already. But after five, someone got in the way, and she wasn't sure anymore. Ernst and Roelof had made their way to the front of the platform. Mr. Liebens was following the judges across the front of the crowd. Number seven chosen. Eight chosen. Passed. Nine chosen; he bowed. Passing, passing, and passing. And then, ten, Clara, was chosen. She curtseyed a thank-you to the judges.

But right then, Mr. Liebens pulled one of the judges aside and started pointing at the back of Clara's canvas. The other two judges came back to join the conversation.

"But this is unfair," Liebens was saying. "This girl's sketch looks better because she's using a forbidden sort of canvas. Is that not true?" The judges disagreed and argued back and forth with him. Ernst and Roelof came forward to listen in. Two of the judges wanted nothing to do with Liebens, but the third had started listening more closely. Liebens was becoming more lively, and his arms cut through the air like an Italian, not a Dutchman. But there was nothing bad about Clara's canvas, and Liebens knew it. He had hoped he could make enough fuss so at the next round the judges would tire enough of him and want to avoid another fight and simply exclude Clara for other reasons.

Ernst realized he had to help, so he moved in beside Mr. Liebens. Just as Mr. Liebens was getting louder than ever and flailing his arms around, Ernst watched Liebens' arms for a moment. The side of Ernst's face could feel the wind from Liebens' hand movements. Ernst counted, four, three, two, one, and then stepped right into the flight of Liebens' arms. Liebens' forearm caught Ernst right across the cheek, and those in the circle gasped as Ernst was hit and staggered against the platform, his head apparently making a very loud thunk noise as it popped against the wooden beams. Ernst crumpled to the ground and moaned a little too loudly, and Mr. Liebens immediately bent down in pity to help the boy.

Roelof stood there stunned for a moment, then he realized that Ernst's foot had hit the platform, not his head. Roelof had seen it a hundred times. Ernst moaned louder and looked at Roelof out of the corner of his eye. The judges made sure the boy was tended to, then they went back to their business. They were glad to be free from the argument with Liebens. Liebens leaned over Ernst, blowing on him to cool him. Roelof turned away from the crowd and quietly said to himself, "I can do that."

The judges had gone on to pull the chestnut horse back in front of the platform. The ten students allowed to advance to the next round pulled their easels in a more uniform line, and the judges started them off with another shout. A tiny bit of Margarieta's tongue stuck out of the corner of her mouth as she sketched, and Clara stared at that horse. It reminded her of the trip from Amsterdam and seeing Liebens on the road coming for them. She wondered if Margarieta had ever really ridden a horse. As she sketched the horse's body, she paid close attention to the shadows made by its muscles. A cathedral had plenty of straight lines, and this made it a bit easier to sketch than a horse. The horse was so much harder to draw that one of the ten student artists just gave up halfway through. He threw his sketch to the ground and stomped off the platform. Only nine were left.

As the sun rose higher and the shadows shortened, the judges finally called time on the second round. Clara's hands were exhausted, but she liked what she had drawn. She didn't even want to lick it. She wished she could see Margarieta's sketch. Clara studied the crowd for any signs of Mother or the uncles. The judges started examining the sketches at the other end and worked their way through just as before, only more quickly now. They did the pointing thing again, but

Clara was less worried this time. Out of the nine, the judges picked Clara, Margarieta, of course, and a very round boy named Gerrit. Mr. Liebens squished his face with his hands and turned away.

The students now had half an hour to mix the colors on their palettes that they would need for the horse and its background. Most of the crowd stayed, but others left for a while. The boy among the three finalists, Gerrit, seemed to be quite alone. He had no one chatting to him between rounds, but through sidelong glances Clara could see that he knew how to mix colors; he moved smoothly. Looking beyond him to Margarieta, Clara watched her pale, jittery hands plod through mental instructions that Clara herself had given her. Clara knew that Margarieta had tremendous painting skills when she concentrated. Her colors might not be perfect, but she could make up for them in the other part.

The color preparation time passed, and all three students were well into their painting. After about a half hour, Mr. Liebens started to walk behind the platform to catch a glimpse of their work, but even before Clara covered her work, the judges had stopped him. Another hour passed. The hot noon sun had given over to the hotter afternoon sun. The students painted carefully, without a word. The perspiration dripped down Gerrit's neck.

But this had gone too far for Liebens. He still had one last move. He stormed off grumbling under his breath, completely abandoning the competition a while, and then he returned to the side of the platform leading two city magistrates. He spoke to them in low tones, and they nodded slowly. Then he called the judges over, and Clara and Ernst knew he was going to try

some new trick. The three students looked a little
nervous, but they were nearly finished with their paintings.

Liebens was insisting that "this" could not continue.
The judges again tried to be patient, waving their fore-
arms like palm branches to cool something down. Finally, Liebens lost control, or pretended to. He moved
away from the judges and stood in the open in front of
the platform and began shouting,

"Are you just going to let this criminal continue?"
he asked the judges, pointing to Clara. "She appears so
innocent, but a barge full of rare and expensive tulips
exploded this morning, as you all now know." He
breathed in and out in the silence. "And this Clara girl
was the one responsible! The captain of the ship—a
good friend and laborer of mine for many years—has
informed me that this morning she left a package there
and ran off. I owned that barge, and for some reason
she has despised me and sought my ruin. On top of
that, she owns a very rare bulb, one of the rarest tulips
in Utrecht, and I believe that she must have been trying to make it more scarce by destroying a bargeload
of others. My ship is gone. My tulips are gone. And
she's still allowed to take part in this art competition.
This is a travesty of justice!" Clara stared for a moment,
then went back to painting feverishly, without missing
a beat.

Liebens walked over to the magistrates. "Would you
please arrest this girl? You have heard Otto's witness
and that of his shipmates. We could even ask her ac-
complices." He walked toward Ernst. "You there. Did
your sister go to the barge and deliver a package this
morning shortly before the barge exploded?"

Ernst's face was red. His eyes darted back and forth

between Liebens and Clara. "You made her do it!" he said. "You made her take that tulip! She didn't do anything!"

"Ah, yes," said Liebens, "the ever-protective brother lying for his sister. But notice, even he admits she was at the barge, and you can see his own hostility to me." He looked back at Ernst. "And why would I blow up my own barge? My own flowers?" Ernst was silent. He wanted to say "because you're an evil Judas," but he held his tongue. Gerrit and Margarieta stood stunned, but Clara continued to paint amidst all of this.

Liebens glanced at Roelof, but then thought better of asking him anything. But Roelof didn't understand whether what was going on was good or bad. For all he knew, Mr. Liebens could be happy about the explosion. Liebens turned away from the boy. But Roelof suddenly spoke up.

"Clara took a bomb to the boat," Roelof said quietly. Ernst seemed to jump away from him.

"What did you say, son?" asked Liebens, turning back.

"Clara took a red and white bomb to the barge," said Roelof, proud of getting the word right.

"She took a bomb, did she? That's right. That's right isn't it?" Liebens said, finding a pearl of great price. Roelof nodded and smiled at Clara. Clara stopped painting and finally spoke up.

"My cousin Roelof calls tulips *bombs*. He's confused," she said. The crowd started to titter, and Liebens laughed with exaggeration. Even the magistrates smiled. They signaled for Clara to come with them.

"But wait," she said. Clara started telling the magistrates the whole story about her father's letters, Liebens demands, and his locking her in his office. But all of it sounded so empty and hollow now. Who would believe it? Then she remembered. She hopped down from the platform and pulled Liebens' last letter from her skirt pocket. She had given Otto the copy she had made.

"Here," she said, "Read this." She held it up for the magistrates and judges to read. The older men squinted and read it. Then their eyes turned back to Liebens.

"Is this your writing?" said a magistrate.

Liebens came over laughing as if it were some pesky joke. He grabbed the letter from Clara's hands and stared at it. *Dear Clara, I don't suspect you'll ever read this note before I get back. But if you do somehow, the key leads to the letter. To get the letter, you must take this tulip to the van Mander barge waiting at the end of the Niewegracht canal. Bring all my notes, and a man there named Otto will trade you for your father's letter.*

"How did you get this?" Liebens asked too quickly. "Where's Otto?" Then he shifted gears too late. "This must be some sort of trick. She's lying," but his voice was too full of panic.

The two magistrates looked at each other, then one said, "You need to come with us, Mr. Liebens." They stepped over to him and firmly gripped his arms. They walked him away, while he kept arguing.

"But what about the competition?" one of the judges asked the magistrates.

"Let it go on. It has nothing to do with this," said a magistrate. Clara climbed back on to the platform and stood behind her painting. *Come on, come on, come on,* she said in her mind. The three competition judges put their heads together again and could find no reason to stop the contest. Even if Liebens were guilty, Margarieta hadn't cheated in the competition. They were the judges of that.

After a few moments, they turned to the three student artists, and the white-haired judge asked, "Students, have you completed your artwork?" The students nodded. "Then please turn your easels around for us all to see them." The easel legs skidded a bit here and there, but finally all three paintings were turned around. But instead of polite applause there was a funeral silence.

Gerrit's painting of the horse was quite beautiful, and Margarieta's horse was even more stunning. Her background displayed a garden full of Soomerschoon crimson, all of it perfectly balanced with spike oil. But Clara hadn't painted the horse at all. She had completely ignored her original horse sketch and had instead painted over it a magnificent, richly colored, carefully detailed—*beached whale*. Its craft was far superior to the others. It showed a wonderful grasp of *houding*. Clara stood there with the broadest smile. Most people stood around with creases of confusion over their faces, even Ernst.

Clara stepped forward. "I get third place, then, don't I? Of the three, mine is the worst painting of a horse, isn't it?" Everyone still stood silently. "Third place. That means I get that chestnut horse for a week, right?" The judges shrugged but seemed almost to nod. "Good," she said. She straightened her skirts. Her voice had the smooth assurance of royalty. "Because I've got to go get my father." She hopped off the platform, and the horse's owner helped her onto the chestnut horse.

# CHAPTER ELEVEN

# Friar's Arms

Clara sat atop the chestnut horse and waited for someone to object—anyone. Ernst stared up at her from a
distance, as if Clara were a guest from another land.
Ernst knew she was headed to Arnhem, but no one
else did. The owner of the horse knew Clara's family
well, and he gave Clara some last-minute pointers. Then
he helped clear away some of the crowd in front of her.

Clara called for Ernst, and he and Roelof came over
and stood by her dangling foot. She didn't want any of
the grown-ups to get in the way of her plan, but the
crowd was noisy anyway. Clara leaned over to Ernst
and spoke in a whisper. "You've got to find the uncles
and Momma," she said. Ernst nodded his head. So did
Roelof. "And tell the uncles to race to the town I told
you about—Arnhem." She spoke it clearly.

Ernst saluted Clara, and Roelof saluted Ernst, for
some reason. Clara looked ahead of her and nudged
the horse to start walking. The horse moved slowly,
with the crowd parting further as she rode away. Clara
longed to get out of the city and ride fast—the wind
against her face—like she had from Amsterdam.

Ernst came out into the space cleared by Clara and
shouted, "That's my sister!" She waved back at him.
Not to be outdone, Roelof came forward, waving his
rubbery wrist. "Good-bye, Princess!" he called at the
top of his lungs. And then he realized he didn't have a

clue about what was going on and asked, "Where is she going?"

Ernst didn't waste another moment. He grabbed Roelof's hand, and they started to run back home in search of the uncles.

The town of Arnhem was the only thing on Clara's mind as she made her way toward Utrecht's south gate, Tolsteegpoort. She had never been to Arnhem before, but that's where Father was still waiting; she was sure. She imagined him lying in a bed of hay, breathing slowly, in a dark stable of some monastery. He had spoken of the monks at Arnhem. But who were they? He hadn't mentioned the name of a monastery or a hospice or a church. It all seemed so far away. Father had left by ship and sailed south, all around Spain to the Mediterranean and then up the Adriatic to the city of Venice, the color capital of the world. For some reason, he had returned by land, through Paris, ending up in Arnhem.

Within a short time, she passed the gate and rode out into the farmland; the odors of stone and fish had been replaced by young wheat and baking soil. Clara turned her nose side to side to try and catch a whiff of linseed. But it wasn't growing on that side of town, so she just imagined it. Amid fields of grain, she and the horse raced by perfectly square fields, crammed with tulips in mathematical rows, a checkerboard of purples, yellows, reds, and whites. When she stared straight ahead, these fields became rivers of rainbows flowing by left and right.

After a while, though, the horizon changed. She could see the farmland patterns giving way to more wildish greens. Between the farmlands that wrapped the towns were the wilder places, waiting for farms, wilder places that might be full of gypsies or robbers or soldiers marching to fight in Germany. She slowed the horse, assuring herself that the animal was tired. She looked back over her shoulder in the hope of seeing some sign of the uncles. No road dust was billowing up behind a carriage.

Clara looked ahead and found an open grassy area next to a creek. There was still a mile or two of farmland between her and the wilds. The creek flowed into the canal that paralleled the road she was on. She dismounted and led the horse to a nice patch of grass by the creek. As she sat there, she realized that she didn't know the horse's name. She rubbed his neck as he stooped to drink from the creek.

"So what's your name?" she asked. She waited for an answer, lightly puckering her lips in thought. "Hmmm, you have very theatrical shadows. Should I call you Caravaggio? Or Manfredi?" The horse moved his head over to some grass. "Or Rubens. Maybe just Paul—Mr. Paul? No, those won't do." She traced her fingers in a small eight shape on his side. "You have so many browns. I think I'll call you *Venice. Mr. Venice.* Yes, that will do." She said the name over and over and imagined the horse smiling at this.

She led the horse back up to the road and studied it for uncles. Nothing. She looked back toward the wilds. "We're just not riding through those wilds alone," she said to the horse. She slowly climbed up on the horse and said those words again, staring at the distant trees. She nudged the horse, and Mr. Venice started moving toward the wilds. "We're not riding through those wilds" she said again, as she made the horse pick up its pace. Soon they were at a slow gallop and then at a full sprint straight toward the dark green wilds, coming closer and closer, all the while Clara shouting louder and louder, "We're not riding through the wilds! We're not riding through the wilds!" She closed her eyes just before passing the first edge of brush and overhanging trees, and through her eyelids, she could tell the sunlight had been replaced by dark shades.

Snapping open her eyes in fear of low branches, she saw the shadowed dirt road wide before her. For a half-mile ahead, no gypsy carriages or troops lined the road. She didn't want to tire Mr. Venice too quickly, but she had to keep going. She could no longer say "We're not riding through the wilds," so she switched to the first catechism question under her breath—"What is your only comfort in life and death? That I am not my own . . . ." After saying it five times, the shadows grew lighter and lighter, and in an instant horse and girl burst out of the dark brush into more open land and sunshine. Clara closed her eyes for a moment and enjoyed the sunlight on her cheeks.

In the hours that passed, the land switched back and forth from brush and wooded areas to open land. Clara stopped several times to rest and water Mr. Venice, but these were always very open areas, where she could see long distances in every direction. Over the hours, only two merchant carriages passed her from the opposite direction, but they showed no interest in this crazy girl out in the middle of the wilds. They had kept their eyes straight ahead without even a nod. Yet Clara sensed that the air got thicker and harder to breathe even in the flat open areas the further she got from Utrecht; she felt herself suffocating in open sunshine with the realization that she was too far to turn back. It was as if she were on a ship in the middle of the largest ocean, with no harbor in any direction.

After resting Mr. Venice for the seventh time, they soon came to a bend in the road that gave her a glimpse of rather different surroundings far ahead. Though the land was flat, the bend where they stopped was just a bit higher, and Clara could just make out lines of buildings, especially a church steeple, in the distance. She could also see, though, that between her and this town, stood the largest forest she would have to pass through yet. She looked at the forest for open breaks, but there were none. Her arms became cold and tingly. That town had to be Arnhem, she assured herself. *But still one last forest.*

Her whole body ached from head to toe after riding for so many hours. Her muscles felt like a mix of stiff iron and oozing porridge. She rubbed the back of her neck and tried not to pay attention to the sun getting closer and closer to the horizon. Clara patted the horse's neck and took a deep breath. "Time to swim through one last sea, Mr. Venice." And they were off. Within moments the coolness of the forest overtook them like a wave, and the late afternoon sunlight barely showed through the canopy of leaves and branches.

Clara slowed the horse down from a full gallop this time, because she remembered that he would have to last the whole forest. There would be nowhere to stop and rest. Every once and a while, Clara twisted her head around to look for anyone coming up behind her in the shadows. Her eyes shot to every noise in the wood, and everything echoed a little louder than before.

Suddenly she pulled Mr. Venice to a dead stop. She looked left and right down a fork in the road. No signs showed which road led to Arnhem. Her fast riding had hidden many sounds in the forest, but as she waited there, the noises came alive. Her head snapped around in every direction. Then she heard voices, a whole group of voices in the distance.

She couldn't wait. She looked at the dirt roads before her, and one looked wider and more trodden than the other. That must be the road to a town like Arnhem. And it was away from the voices. She kicked Mr. Venice into action down that road, but the road suddenly started to bend. She followed it for another few moments, then she slowed a bit. The voices were getting louder. She had ridden right toward them.

She brought the horse to a full stop. Listening for words, she noticed the voices sounded a bit angry with one another. She couldn't make out the words at all. But it didn't have the rhythms of Dutch. Then just around the bend in front of her she saw horses and the edge of a faded red carriage. In an instant, she turned her horse around and sprinted back toward the fork in the road. The voices behind her shifted into shouts, but she didn't look back. She kept riding along the bends in the road as near to full speed as she could get. The voices didn't get any fainter, and she could feel the movement of other horses behind her.

When she came to the fork in the road, she prepared Mr. Venice to turn. The other road was narrower but straighter, and she would be able to race the horse faster. She slowed Mr. Venice, and he turned like he understood the plan. Then he raced at full charge. They sped like this for at least two miles without slowing, and without noticing that the voices had long vanished. Finally, she eased up and listened—no voices, no horses. But now she wondered if she were even headed toward Arnhem. For all she knew, this road could be taking her back to Utrecht. She didn't stop though; she had to get out of this forest. Clara leaned forward, tired, resting her body against the horse's neck as he padded along slowly. Then she heard them again.

Horses. She heard the gallop of horses racing up the road behind her. No voices, just horses tied together jangling, and Clara came back to life, pushing Mr. Venice faster and faster through the trees. She slowed once and then again, but each time the rush of horses became louder. She glanced over her shoulder and caught the silhouette of a carriage in the distance. Mr. Venice was too tired to go any faster, but she pushed him just a bit more, hoping for a sign of more light and the end of the forest. She turned to look back again, and she had a full view of the dark carriage shape, with what looked like one driver. She checked over her shoulder and now she could tell that he had a clear view of her, and he was yelling and picking up speed to catch her. He wasn't anyone she knew.

Clara studied the road ahead of her and saw a bend approaching. She could no longer outrace him. She had to get off the horse and hide. Even though the carriage was gaining, she had to slow before the bend. The beat of the carriage horses pressed against her ears, but once around the bend, she slowed enough to slide off Mr. Venice. She tumbled into a thick patch of bright green ferns. But Mr. Venice just stopped on the road above her. She had wanted him to go on ahead and not give her spot away. She tried to wave him on, but he just stared one eye at her waving hand.

In less than a count of ten, the air exploded with the sounds of horse and carriage at top speed, and Mr. Venice had to dart to the side as the carriage tried to blow by. But the road was too narrow, and the horses collided with Mr. Venice as the carriage driver did everything he could to stop his team. Everything was horses squealing, humans shouting, wheels bouncing, and bushes scratching. The forest seemed to sigh when everything finally stopped moving. Down in the ferns, Clara watched through her fingers and saw that Mr. Venice was standing safely down off the road. The carriage had landed halfway off the road, tilted at an odd angle, but not overturned. The driver tried to coax the horses back on to the road, when the carriage door opened, facing up into the sky because of the carriage's odd angle. Someone was pulling himself up to the door opening.

She watched but the person couldn't pull himself up all the way. Then she heard him call.

"Clara!"

She sat up. He called again. She stood this time, still not believing her ears.

"Clara!" He called again louder. "You fool girl, where are you?!"

She stumbled up from the ferns and called back. "Uncle Caspar? Is that you?"

"Yes, of course, it is. Who else would be so stupid?" The carriage driver had been struggling with the horses, and finally he drove them all the way back onto the road. The uncles inside grunted loudly as the carriage made its way back to level ground.

Uncle Hendrick stuck his head out of the side of the carriage. "Excuse me, miss, but have you seen a crazy, fool young lady riding that way?"

Uncle Caspar stuck his head out too. "You'd recognize her easily. She'd be the one *without* the Manfredi painting under her arm."

"Ah, yes," Clara said, glancing back from where she had come. "That girl passed me grumbling about how slow carriages were these days. I didn't want anything to do with her. She looked nasty, like a Pharaoh in lace."

The uncles got out of the carriage, holding their stiff backs. They each hugged Clara and then introduced their driver. Clara, in turn, introduced them to Mr. Venice. It was growing darker, and they started off again on the last few miles to Arnhem, with Mr. Venice tied alongside the carriage.

The uncles described their journey, mentioning the yelling gypsies in the red carriage that had passed them a few miles back. Then they turned serious and tried to prepare Clara for what she might find in Arnhem. They couldn't bring themselves to say it, so Clara would finish their sentences. Yes, she assured them, she knew that Father may not be there, or he may have the plague, or he may already be dead. She was ready.

When they finally arrived at Arnhem, the ride into town was a blur. Clara hopped out of the carriage before it was fully stopped and grabbed the first person she came upon.

"Where are the monks?" she asked an old woman. The woman was creased and yellow, and she was taken aback by Clara. She waved three fingers down the city road to the left, down the road where the twilight shadows faded. Another woman she asked looked confused and pointed her a slightly different direction, but to a specific building. Clara stood silently for a while staring at the building down the street. People crossed back and forth between her and the building. The small thatch-gray house seemed to grow bigger, taking over everything between it and Clara. The uncles' carriage stood behind her.

Then Clara hitched up her skirts and started jogging, then running toward the round-edged house. A knee-high wall of yellow tulips stretched itself around the gray walls. She ran to the door and started banging on it. The uncles got out of the carriage and stood beside her. No one answered the door. Clara let the uncles take over banging the door, while she stood, hands on hips. Finally they tried to open the door, but it was bolted.

When they started banging again, a bear-sized man came running around from the back of the house. He was waving his hands but wouldn't speak; his monk's robe became all bunched up at the arms. Clara ran up to him.

"Please, sir, my father is inside. I must see him." But the man didn't talk. He signaled for them to stop pounding on the door. That looked like the only thing he was interested in. Then he signed for them to go away.

"These must be monks under a vow of silence," said Uncle Caspar out of the side of his mouth.

"Please, please, sir, show me my father," Clara started clinging to his wide sleeve, as he started toward the back of the building.

The monk tried to sign something new. His hands pointed to the sky and then made circles, then he flapped his arms like wings and made his hands a horn and blew it without noise.

Uncle Hendrick said, "I think he's saying that the birds should learn to play the horn."

"Well that's not very informative," said Uncle Caspar. "We already knew that."

"Perhaps," said Hendrick, "he's not a very bright monk, and he's trying to teach us the alphabet." The monk shook his head and moved his arms more violently. Clara tried to decipher his moves.

"I know," said Hendrick, "He wants to know if we flew here. Oh, I told you he was an idiot."

Finally, the monk shouted at them, "No! No! No! I was telling you to come back in the morning, when the sun returns and the rooster crows." The uncles stared as though they had broken something.

"I thought you weren't supposed to speak," said Uncle Caspar.

"No, that's just my way of getting visitors to leave me alone. Most people give up and walk away, but no, not you with the smarty mouths."

"I say," said Hendrick, "do you usually insult visitors?"

"Only when they're stupid," said the man. "Now leave us alone." He started to walk away, grumbling. Clara started begging him again, but he snapped around.

"Look, this is a hospice. We've got people dying inside there. Some have the plague. Can't you just let them go in peace? That's our job. You'll just stir them into a frenzy, and then we'll have to spend the whole night calming their fears. I am peace and light to them, and you're not going to muck that up."

"You're certainly a 'sunshine fairy,'" said Uncle Hendrick under his breath.

"What was that?" the monk shot back, squaring his shoulders.

"I said, 'York mainly has some fine dairies.'"

"Get out of here," said the monk. "Come back in the morning," and he walked off. Clara resigned and went and sat on the front step. But Uncle Caspar couldn't hold it in any longer, and he started making a louder and louder noise as though he were going to jump a hurdle.

"Just be patient, Uncle Caspar, the monk is right," his niece said. He glared at Clara and then bolted off behind the house after the monk, making a dog noise. Uncle Hendrick ran after him. There were shouts from around the side of the house, and Clara put her face on her knees, not caring. A moment later, the monk came staggering out from the side with Uncle Caspar hanging on his back, gripping the monk's neck. The monk dragged a gasping Uncle Hendrick along the ground by the collar of his jacket.

Clara ignored them for a while as they wrestled, then she shouted, "No fits. Fits get you nothing," citing her mother. The monk flicked Uncle Caspar from side to side, trying to get him off his back, and finally, Caspar flopped in the dirt. The monk held apart his arms and tipped forward, flopping on Uncle Caspar.

"Father's not here," Clara said quietly. She just knew. And she got up off the step and started wandering down the street. The driver in the carriage looked bored too, so he started to turn the horse carriage to follow her. She gave him the sign to wait there.

Clara wandered up and down too many streets to count. The sun was getting lower and lower. She sat in several squares and watched the people, hoping to catch a glance of Father down some alley. She walked around the inside walls of Arnhem. She was hungry, but she didn't notice.

Finally she headed for the burial yard by the old church. She had passed it several times, but now it all began to make sense to her. She hadn't been brought here to be a Solomon, winning all of Abraham's land. She had been brought here like Moses, to see the promised land from a distance. It wasn't her place to enjoy

Father again. It was hers to see and rest. She walked on, convincing herself that that wasn't so bad. Moses had wandered for decades and never received the promised land. God was kind, though He chastened Moses for faithlessness. Not everyone gets to be a Joshua, and she had no right.

She came to the edge of the burial yard and looked for a fresh mound of dirt. She made her way through the crosses and statues, graves of husbands and wives, graves of children, soldiers and maids, grandmothers and pastors. They were all here; they each had their stories. They had their rest.

Finally, she saw it. There it was on the far edge. Pale twilight haze lit the fresh mound of dirt. It looked like any new grave. It grew larger as she walked up to it. The dirt was piled up higher than the ground to make room for the body beneath. Here must be her promised land. Here was her father's resting place. And hers too. She didn't cry as she ran her hand over the crumbly dirt. Father had taught her from afar. He had taught her through Momma, through the uncles, through the Soomerschoon. And it was better this way. How could she explain giving away his color secrets to Liebens like they were trash? He would have forgiven her, but she didn't have to see his sad face now. She couldn't bear to sadden his face.

That spring evening was warm, and she stretched out her body and lay next to the mound for a few moments. She smiled as she dozed, remembering that day, the barge, Otto, sketching the cathedral, the muscles of the horse, the creek, the wild woods, her father's face from long ago.

◆   ◆   ◆

Hours later a soft hand shook her. "Please, miss," a boy's
voice said. "You can't stay here." Clara tried to wake
and rub away her sleep. It was deeply dark, and there
were two boys—no they were older girls—trying to
wake her. Clara sat up, and the girls raised her to her
feet. They kept insisting on getting out of the cemetary.
They didn't like it there, they said. Clara was walking
before she could see, but when her eyes cleared, she
could see the young ladies were only two or three years
older than herself. Their clothes stood out as lights in
the darkness, and they wore common maids' clothes.
Clara kept asking questions, but they just helped her
along. They didn't answer, but perhaps, Clara thought,
she was speaking nonsense sleep-talk.

After a long walk, the girls walked her through the
back door of a kitchen, a kitchen whose evening aro-
mas lingered faintly—onions, beef, rye bread. The food
had been cleared away for hours, but their shadows
were still here. The maids took her through a candlelit
hallway, and at the end, there waited a tall man in a
long robe who was lighting a fat candle. Clara was awake
now, but not sure enough to question or object. The
maids turned her over to the man, who ever so gently
led her down another hall. He wouldn't answer her
questions either. They went up a flight of stone stairs,
and this man handed her over to another, who also
seemed to be waiting. He was much older, and his candle
made his eyes sparkle. He smiled and held out his soft
hand. She followed without a word. They walked
around a broad rectangular ledge that overlooked an
ornate floor and sat under a tall, arched roof. This was
no thatched house.

The man led her to a door, and he stood there silently for a moment, as if catching his breath from the

walk. Clara stared into his eyes, seeking what was next. He opened the door slowly and pointed in with his smile. Clara tilted her head to look through the door, and the old man whispered as she passed him, "We were told to watch for you." Clara was angry for a moment that she was dreaming. She stared down the long hall and tried to make out objects from the fading candles that lined the long walls. She glanced back at the old man, and he waited there, silently urging her on.

She walked with soft steps over the stone, farther and farther into the hall. They could have fit two ships end to end inside of this hall. The old man and the door were far behind her now. Then Clara stopped and covered her mouth. She could see the four beds at the far end of the hall and started walking faster, then running, her steps making echoes along the walls.

As she came to the four beds, three were empty and clean. One was full. Her stomach felt like she was swinging down on a long swing as she felt her way around the bed to the man lightly snoring. She knew those snores, and no music could match them. She got down on her knees and just stared at the lines on her father's face. *What is man that you are mindful of him?* She ran her fingers over his eyebrows and drew a figure eight in his pale hair. Father shifted in his blanket, then opened his eyes. He had seen her so many times in his dreams that he didn't know if this was another. But a copy is never like the original. He reached out his hand and touched her nose. She rested her cheek on his arm.

Father opened his mouth and whispered to Clara, "I knew you wouldn't give up."

# CHAPTER TWELVE

# Bethel's Oil

Morning brought a very bright fog. The sun lit the mist but hid itself behind the moist veil. Clara and the uncles stood next to the carriage at the bottom of a long line of steps and waited as two friars helped Father hobble down them. Father was taller than both of them, his wide brimmed hat clearing their tonsured heads. Beneath his hat hung long blond locks, not gray, and a blond beard that he didn't have when he left. The friars and Father mused that what they were doing was probably more dangerous than just letting Father walk. If one tripped, all three would tumble down.

Finally they came to the carriage. Mr. Venice had been added to help pull up front. Father thanked his two friar friends and kissed them on both cheeks, Venetian style. They patted him gently on the back. Clara held his hand, steadying him to the carriage door.

Then he turned back to the friars and held up Clara's hand. "See, this is what I was talking about."

"Don't start again," said one of the friars, groaning at first, then chuckling.

"But don't forget it," Father said. "No Franciscan will be a good painter until you have women in your life. A wife to hold and a daughter to admire."

"We have Mary, the Mother of God," offered the other friar, in a way that showed he'd said it many times to Father.

"No. Joseph had the real Mary. You just have a ghostly idea of her, sitting far away on a throne. That won't make great paintings. You need real women, I tell you," Father said.

"Take him home please, Clara," said the friar.

"Go away," said the other with mock tiredness. "Remember, you're a sick man."

"Was, was, was a sick man," Father said. He turned back to the carriage, but as he stooped to get in, he bumped the side of the door with his elbow and pretended it was his head. Clara gasped and reached to touch him.

"Got you," he said and climbed in.

She shook her head like Mother. "That's where he got it," she said quietly.

The ride back to Utrecht was calm; the sunshine burned off all the fog. The uncles sat together on one side of the carriage, facing Father and Clara on the other. The three pressed Father for the tale of his adventure, a story he would have to tell again and again when he got back home. Then Clara made the uncles explain what happened with their wrestling match over at the hospice. Uncle Caspar said he had been more bored than angry and needed the exercise after sitting in the carriage for so long. Uncle Hendrick still complained about the nasty nature of that monk. Father said he thought the monks over at the hospice were Dominicans, and that was supposed to explain it.

Clara kept steering the conversation away from her adventures. At some point she would have to tell Father about how she had ruined his color business by giving away the spike oil and crimson secrets. Not now, though. That morning she had awakened when she heard a rooster crow. When it crowed the second time, she knew she was the Peter who betrayed her father's trust. *What would he do now? He would be just another color merchant. Nothing special anymore.* As she stared out the carriage windows onto the passing green wilds, it was as if some part of her mind would pop up with explanations that made her look good. But she was beyond that now. She knew she had given away some of those secrets in spite. She had foolishly believed Liebens' lie that Father was in town.

Her mind reentered the carriage as Father was explaining how, on his way through France, he hurt his leg when he fell from his horse in the rain. Then he had picked up a fever he had feared would turn into the plague. The Franciscans had taken him in and doctored him through his feverish days.

The arrival of Father back home was like the best fireworks. The whole Pekstokken parish filled the street in front of their house. Mother hung around Father's neck like a new bride, biting his ears and kissing every part of his face. Ernst and Roelof did cartwheels in the street as best they could. Everyone had to hear his story. Neighbors filled the house with food and wine, enough to last for weeks.

Around their table that night, the family was exhausted from laughing and eating. Uncle Hendrick kept trying to justify to his wife, Aunt Griet, the necessity of his helping Caspar wrestle that monk, but she kept poking holes in his explanations with simple questions.

Father pulled his nephew Roelof onto his lap. "I'm almost as tall as Ernst," Roelof said.

"I believe you're right, Mr. Hodge-Podge," said Father.

"Did you bring me anything?" Roelof asked. Aunt Griet was appalled and apologized. Everyone else laughed it off.

"I did pick up something nice from Venice for you, but—I'm sorry to say—when I was thrown from the horse, I lost all the gifts I was bringing. I'm your only gift," Father said, exaggerating with his arms.

Roelof thought about this for a moment. "Will you go back and get that thing you dropped?" Laughs burst out, and Roelof frowned around at them.

"He doesn't get any of this," Ernst said.

"I doooo," insisted Roelof, getting the insult.

"Then where has my father been?" said Ernst.

"Riding a horse," Roelof said. "Dropping stuff."

As the candles burned down, no one wanted to leave or go to bed. Everyone kept eating bits of food here and there to stay awake. The question of Mr. Liebens came up, and Mother said she had received word that day that he had been formally charged by the magistrates with endangering the community by blowing up his barge. But it seemed that people were far more angry with him for blowing up all those tulips than possibly hurting any people. The men on the boat confessed to being hired by Liebens to blow it up as a last-ditch way to win the Manfredi, win praise for his own teaching, and win higher prices for his hidden tulips. Liebens was fired from the orphanage and would be spending his time paying large amounts of restitution to several big tulip merchants in Amsterdam.

All that news quieted things down, bringing back bad memories too soon. Mother stood up as if she'd just remembered something and went upstairs. A minute later she walked down carrying a framed painting draped with a throw cloth. She leaned it against the fireplace and didn't say a thing for a moment. All eyes were looking at her for explanations.

"I got it," said Mother. Several people asked, what?

She walked back to the painting in high fashion, and as she slowly removed the cloth from it, Clara was mentally fitting the colors and shapes of the Manfredi to it. But when the cloth was gone, the Manfredi expectations dissolved into her beached whale painting. The uncles cheered. Clara pinked. Father hadn't yet seen the painting that had set him free. He moved closer to it and stared. Clara wanted to lick it. She was all done with her own painting hopes. They were things of the past.

"Shouldn't it have been the Manfredi?" she asked, not really knowing what to say. "Isn't that the way things are supposed to go? Something about Margarieta feeling so bad that she gives up her painting for me?" But none of this was said seriously. She certainly didn't think she deserved it. As she spoke, Clara realized that she had even lost respect for the Manfredi. It too was just a frozen copy of the world. Not real art. Father kept examining the beached whale painting.

Clara picked up Roelof and walked him around the room. "Now this is *real* art," she said, looking into Roelof's face. The two of them walked slowly out of the room and out to the kitchen. She set Roelof on a table.

"So what should we do tomorrow?" she asked Roelof.

"No more walking, please, Princess," he said. She laughed and pushed his bangs from his forehead.

"No. No more *Princess*. Just *Clara*. Got it?"

"Yes, Princess," he said. She put her hands on her

hips in a mock rebuke. Roelof rolled his head around and said, "Clara, Clara, Clora, Clira, Cloora, Colora, Cilera—" until she put her hand over his mouth. He licked it.

After a while, Clara wanted to be alone. So she convinced Roelof to go back to his parents. She headed out to the color shop and sat by herself for a long while. In the other room, Father wondered where she was and gimpily made his way into the color shop and leaned against a post. He stared at her without speaking. She knew he wanted to know what was wrong. He waited.

"The uncles don't know," she began. "No one else knows." She paced around a bit. "I've been an Apostle Peter to you." Father rubbed his beard, trying to make this out.

Then he exaggerated a sigh. "You mean, while I was away you became the Pope? That's horrible. Does the pastor know about this?" She suppressed a smile and waved him off.

"I'm serious," she said.

"May I wear your pointy-hat some time?" he asked.

"I gave away some of your color secrets," she said. Father's smile faded, and Clara's heart raced.

"Which ones?" he said.

"I was mad at you. I thought you were here in Utrecht, tricking us. And Liebens wouldn't give me the letter. But I didn't really have to give the secrets, I know. I was proud. I'm very, very sorry. I'm such a Judas."

"Which ones?" Father asked again, no smile.

"I used some of your crimson notes and that spike oil thing," she said. There was a long silence.

"I don't care," Father smiled. "You saved me. How could you think I would be angry?"

"I knew you'd forgive me, but still, I've ruined everything. I killed your business. I didn't want to see your face fall because of me. I know how you love your color work."

"You're thinking of the wrong persons. All the wrong people." He walked toward her and pulled her head into his side. "You're neither a Peter nor a Judas. You're a Jacob. You served a Laban and bought off an Esau with those recipes. Those are good and holy things." He stared off. "How does it go?" Father searched his memory. "'Your name shall no longer be called Jacob, but Israel; for you have struggled with God and with men and have prevailed.' What more could a father want?"

She couldn't speak for a moment. She just buried her head in his side.

"Let's see," he said. "'Jacob' and 'Clara' have two syllables each. 'Israel' has three. 'Jacob is to 'Israel' as 'Clara' is to, uh, 'Clisrael?'" They both laughed. "Pretty bad poetry, eh?" he asked. She nodded.

"You won't really call me that will you?" she asked, wiping her tears.

"Only when you're good," he said. She nudged his arm. "But we need an altar for you."

"A what?" Clara said.

"An altar. You know, a memorial like Jacob made. He poured oil on it," he said.

"I bet it wasn't linseed oil," she said offhandedly.

"That's it!" he said. "Your altar can be your whale painting. It's covered in linseed oil. And it was painted where you wrestled." Clara smiled and shrugged her shoulders.

"You know what else?" Father said. "Wait. First, as much as we like to joke around here, you've got to know that I would never trick you like that, hiding out while my family suffered. I'd never do that.

"But I was also going to say that you haven't even ruined my color business." Clara looked up. "No, no. That crimson. It had its time. But that's not the favorite color anymore. Venice thinks it's a bit overused now. It will still be big in the Netherlands for a few years, but in *the* color capital, the hot color is—are you ready?" She smiled and nodded. He leaned over and whispered. "It's azure blue." He nodded slowly, big-eyed. "And I've got *three* recipes memorized."

"And as for that spike oil trick, well, only your uncles thought it was a secret. They are such blabbermouths that they spill like waterfalls. I told them it was a secret just to slow them down. All the other color merchants in Utrecht know it. We just keep some things away from all the painters for their own good."

"So I'll mix up the azure blue, and then you try it out in a landscape painting or on another whale." Clara gently pulled away from him.

"I don't want to paint anymore, please."

"Now, why not?" Father asked. She walked away in a slow zigzag.

"I don't understand why we do it, I guess," Clara said. "That Soomerschoon I had for a while was pure art. Pure beauty. No matter how good our paintings are, they are always just weak copies."

Father covered his eyes, pretending to faint. "Oh, heresy! blasphemy! And in my own shop." He started pulling on his shirt as if to rip it. She nudged him with her elbow. "I've been away too long," Father said. "What a horrible view of painting you have." He pulled on his beard. "It's not about copying. It's about seeing what others can't see. It's about pointing people to things that they've become numb to. You lived your Soomerschoon inside and out. How few people get to do that? But see the effect it's had on you? Now you could try to capture that unspeakable mystery so others can look at Soomerschoons differently—in a way they've never imagined. And not just flowers. People and history and common things. Especially the common things. We think we know them, and they hide so much mystery inside. It's all lit up, but we miss it."

Father lowered his voice, "Painting can focus our eyes. Of course, very few painters can do that well. You might some day. I can't. But I get to help with colors. That's my joy. And when we ever so rarely find a painting that captures the mystery, that captures what you found out about that Soomerschoon. Then we don't just marvel. We want to bow and cover our mouths."

Clara wiped her nose and stared at him. "Music can do that too," she said.

"Yes," he said, as if she had finally got it. Then he said slowly, "But it's always rare, and it takes great patience."

"*Houding*," she said and looked into Father's eyes.

"*Houding*," he said.

After a long silence, Father asked, "Shall we go back to the others?"

"We shall," and she put her arm in his.

"I bet Mr. Hodge-Podge is asleep," said Father.

"I bet he's eating all the food," said Clara.

"I know," said Father as they walked, hitting upon an idea. "Let's teach him that the words, no the phrase . . ." and he whispered an idea into Clara's ear.

"Oooooh, I don't know," Clara said, slowly shaking her head. "Remember, it was Mr. Hodge-Podge there who said I carried a 'bomb' to the barge. That wasn't much fun."

"Don't go chicken on me now," said Father. "How will he ever be a good artist if we don't mess up his head a bit?"

"Okay," she said, stretching the word over several syllables. "I'm in. It sounds dangerous, but good."

## Acknowledgments:

The early seventeenth-century map of Utrecht displayed on pages eight and nine is used courtesy of the Bancroft Library, University of California Berkeley.

The Soomerschoon image used on the back cover is taken from the tulip book of P. Cos, florist of Haarlem, 1637 and is used with permission of the Wageningen UR Library, Wageningen, The Netherlands (www.agralin.nl/desktop/speccol).

Thanks to all those who helped with fact checking and/or read earlier versions of this story and gave me many helpful comments—my wife Paula, our own kids (Amanda, Chelsea, Mac, and Mr. Eustace Hodge-Podge), my dad and mom, Doug and Anna Jones, my sister Lucy Jones, Doug Wilson, Sandra Haven, Sandy McKay, Susan Gutting, Marie Prys, John Barach, the Helsels, the Schlects, and the Hagopians.

For those interested in pursuing more background of the golden era of Dutch art, the following books are some of those that were especially helpful in writing this story: Benjamin Kaplan, *Calvinists and Libertines*; Sir Charles Eastlake, *Methods and Materials of Painting of the Great Schools and Masters;* Zbigniew Herbert, *Still Life with a Bridle;* Simon Schama, *The Embarrassment of Riches;* Joaneath Spicer and Lynn Federle Orr, *Masters of Light;* Svetlana Alpers, *The Art of Describing;* Paul Taylor, *Dutch Flower Painting.*

The poem Clara recites in chapter one is from the seventeenth-century Dordrecht poet and schoolmaster Pieter van Godewijck.

The painting I had in mind for the children's visit to Van der Ast's house in chapter four was Ambrosius Bosschaert's (1573–1621) *Flowers in a Glass Beaker.* Oil on copper. Norton Simon Foundation.

The three paintings that show up in Liebens' office during Clara's struggle in chapter nine are:

Hendrick Ter Brugghen (1588–1629); *Melancholia* (ca. 1627–28); oil on canvas; Toronto, Art Gallery of Ontario.

Joost Cornelisz Droochsloot (1585–1666); *Saint Martin Dividing His Cloak* (1623); oil on panel; Amsterdam, Rijksmuseum.

Balthasar Van der Ast (1593–1657); *Flowers in a Vase with Shells and Insects* (ca. 1628); oil on panel; London, private collection; National Gallery.

Bartolomeo Manfredi (c.1580–1620) was a noted disciple of Caravaggio (1573–1610) and both were very popular in Utrecht during this time. Until recently, many of Manfredi's works were misattributed to Caravaggio himself. Clara's story never reveals which of Manfredi's paintings was the first-place prize, but many images of his paintings, along with each of the artists above, can be viewed on the internet.